THE HAWKINS' MANOR

SRIJAN MALVIYA

Contents

CHAPTER ONE

Happy Place

Can someone be so obsessed with something that it pushes them over the edge?

They say every house has a story—mine was no exception. Three lives were lost in that place where my family was going to live.

The train glided forward with a gentle rocking motion, its wheels clattering against the tracks in a calming rhythm. Overhead lights cast a warm glow on rows of seats. Time seemed too slow, and the quiet was only broken by a snore or the faint rustle of newspapers. My mind was miles away, spiralling deeper into the secret I carried. I stared out the window, watching the darkening countryside roll by, yet all I could think about was the house.

What little I know, William Hawkins once lived there with his family—his wife, Stella, and their son, Arthur. When their bodies were found lifeless, no one dared to set foot in that house again—but for me, it was the perfect opportunity, a jackpot waiting to be claimed.

I kept this information to myself, and didn't share it with Leslie. Now, I felt the weight of my secret pressing down on me, growing heavier with each passing minute. How could I tell her? It's unlikely she'd understand. She'd panic. She'd want to leave and throw away everything, the house, our future-my future. And I couldn't let that happen. Not after everything I'd sacrificed to buy that mansion. It was my only chance to finally be someone of greater standing.

18th November, 1996
8:00 P.M.

In just two hours, the train will carry us to our final destination. I can hardly wait to see the glittering lights reflected in her eyes and to discover the reactions of my children. A strange mix of nerves and excitement swirls within me—I'm not sure which feeling will win.

Leslie sat beside me. "It's been a while since you've said anything," she murmured, her soft voice breaking the silence. Her hazel eyes searched my face. "What's on your mind?

I couldn't tell her the truth. Not now, never. She'd leave her job. She'd never set foot in that house. I'd be ruined. And for what? For some old tragedy? No. Nothing would stand in my way. Not even the truth.

I clenched my jaw, forcing myself to look away from her trusting eyes. "Nothing serious. Just praying for everything to go smoothly. It's a big step for all of us."

She smiled, resting her head on my shoulder. "Don't worry. Everything will be fine."

I felt a pang of unease, but was I the first person to keep secrets from a partner? Certainly not. So why should I let this guilt weigh me down? Her trust was absolute, but I couldn't afford to let it stop me. Not now. I'd convinced myself that this secret was for her own good. She didn't need to know. She'd be happier that way. For now, I dodged her question—but how much longer can I keep this up? Then, from across the aisle, a voice pierced through the hum of the train.

"New start?"

I looked up, instantly annoyed. It was the woman from seat 101, sitting in front of us. The one who had been watching us since she got on the train in Birmingham. A woman in her fifties, heavyset and overly friendly. It was clear she was wealthy, her attire radiating an effortless elegance. I could tell she had been dying to start a conversation, and now she'd found her chance.

"Sorry to intrude," she continued, leaning forward slightly. "But I heard you mention a new start—are you folks moving somewhere?"

Leslie, ever polite, answered before I could shut her

down. "Oh, yes. We're moving to Whalley. A fresh start for the family."

The woman's eyes lit up, and I could already see the questions forming on her lips. Damn it, why can't people mind their own business?

"That must be exciting!" she gushed. "What's taking you to Whalley?"

Leslie, still smiling, replied, "As a nurse, I've recently been transferred to The Beardwood Hospital, and my husband, Aston, thought it would be best for us to relocate there permanently with our family."

The woman in Seat No. 101 glanced at me with a thin, knowing smile. I realized it was my turn to be interrogated.

"And you are Aston?"

"Yes," I muttered, barely looking at her.

"What do you do, Aston?" she pressed. "Let me guess—Army, right? You look like the type. Strong build, elegant, confident. I bet you're what, forty? Is the height 6'1 or 6'2?"

My teeth grind together. I had no interest in engaging with her or learning anything about her but Leslie, always too open, too kind, jumped in again.

"No, actually," she said with a laugh, "he's thirty six

and works as a journalist for a newspaper."

I didn't want to talk about my job. I didn't want to talk about anything. This woman was too nosy, too intrusive.

Seat No. 101 tilted her head slightly and asked, "That's quite convenient, but what about the children?"

"We've reviewed a few schools in Whalley and plan to shortlist one soon. It's our first time there, so once we settle in, we'll gradually figure everything out. After spending nearly 35 years in Birmingham, we're taking a leap into a town that feels like uncharted territory to us. To be honest, I'm feeling a mix of anxiety and curiosity about what lies ahead. I can't shake the sense that many things will unfold there, and I'll have to see how I respond to it all. For now, I'm just hoping for a simple, normal life."

Seat No. 101 offered a warm smile and said, "Good luck with that. I'll pray to God that everything goes well for you, and that this new place brings joy and prosperity into your life. It's never easy to move in search of a new shelter, and even harder to turn that shelter into a home. But I believe good things are waiting for you and your family." She paused for a moment before her gaze softened. "By the way, I didn't ask—what are the names of these two adorable nippers sleeping next to you?

Leslie smiled fondly and replied, "Her name is Ebba.

She's 16 now and already behaves like a fully grown lady. She's incredibly sharp and dreams of becoming a teacher one day. You'll always find her with her nose buried in a book. And this little one is my son, Liam. Turned 12 last month. A bundle of energy. And honestly, the only reason I'm able to talk to you right now is because he's napping. He's completely his dad's son."

Seat No. 101's smile wavered slightly, touched with a hint of sadness. "You have a sweet family," she breathed. "I once had one, too. My husband is no more, and now it's just my daughter who looks after me. She lives in Birmingham. I'm returning from her place, actually."

Leslie's expression grew gentle. "I'm so sorry to hear about your husband," she said with genuine sympathy. "But it's heartening to know you have such a loving daughter to care for you."

"Thanks."

Leslie hesitated for a moment before asking, "I'm sorry—I didn't even ask your name or what you do.."

"It's all right," she replied gently. "My name is Grace and I work as a legal clerk at the Manchester Crown Court."

"It's really nice meeting you, Grace," Leslie said with a soft smile. "Now I know someone from Whalley, and that gives me a bit of confidence."

Grace's eyes warmed. "You're not alone there, Leslie. If you ever need any kind of help, remember that you have me." She reached into her bag, pulled out a small piece of paper, and scribbled something on it. "Here's my address," she said, handing it over. "You can come by anytime you want."

Leslie took the paper with a grateful nod, tucking it carefully into her purse. "Thank you, Grace. That means a lot."

Our destination had arrived. It was time to step out into our new world and face whatever awaited us. The sound of the train's brakes felt like music to my ears, and this night seemed to hum with the promise of a new beginning.

This was the last station, so every passenger began to disembark. I carried two large suitcases with a duffle bag slung over my shoulder. Leslie held Liam's hand tightly while juggling a leather bag on her right side, and Ebba, still battling her drowsiness, struggled to stand straight.
Grace moved easily with only her handbag. Before parting ways, she turned back toward us, her voice light and warm.

"I'm looking forward to catching up with you soon," she said, smiling. "I'd love to visit and help you settle in. By the way, I didn't ask—where are you staying?"

Leslie turned to me with a curious smile. "I'm not sure about the exact address," she admitted. "He wanted to keep it a surprise. But there's a name for the house... What was it, Aston?"

"It's no secret," I replied calmly. "I just didn't want to talk about the house before we got there." I paused, the weight of my thoughts lingering. Better to say nothing than to lie, I reasoned. That house had its past, and I didn't want it overshadowing my present.

Grace gave me a small, understanding nod. "I get it. It's okay if you don't want to tell me."

"It's **The Hawkins' Manor**," I finally said.

Her reaction was immediate. "What?" she blurted, her voice rising sharply. Her mouth fell open, eyebrows shooting up in disbelief.

For a moment, she seemed frozen; her face draining of colour as if every drop of blood had left it. I couldn't quite place it—shock, fear, or something else—but there was no mistaking how unnerved she suddenly looked.

"What's wrong?" I inquired, my tone calm yet tense.

She stood there, staring at me with an expression I couldn't quite read—disbelief, maybe, or something darker. After a brief pause, she finally spoke. "I hope you know what you're doing. God bless your family."

I froze, trying to make sense of her words, to

understand what she was really saying. Before I could respond, she turned to Leslie with a look of pity—eyes soft, almost sorrowful—then turned and walked away, disappearing into the night beyond the station.

Leslie frowned, her voice low but sharp. "What was that? What did she mean?"

"Trust me, I'm still trying to figure it out," I replied, my thoughts tangled.

Leslie shook her head. "Weird, don't you think?"

"That lady's weird, that's all," I said, forcing calm into my voice. "No need to overthink it. It's an important night for us."

I tried to control the moment, to calm the tension creeping in around us, but deep down, her words clung to me like a shadow.

My wife tends to over-analyse things. I know she'll dwell on what Grace said, and no matter how much I want to, I can't stop her. All I can do is hope that when we finally reach our new home, she steps inside without lingering doubts or fears.

We stood on the main road, waiting for some form of transportation. The clock had already struck 11:00 P.M., and the streets were empty. I didn't think we'd find anything at this hour. After waiting for what felt like forever—30 long minutes—we had no choice but to start walking east. A slim passageway bordered by towering trees on either side.

The broker had told me it was about a 45-minute walk from the station to the manor, but I wasn't sure how we'd manage. Leslie looked drained, her energy spent on a conversation she'd barely understood, and my two children—practically living zombies—stumbled forward, eyes half-shut, fighting to stay awake.

Just as I was about to give up hope, I spotted a figure sprinting toward us from a distance. A boy, waving his arms frantically. He stopped in front of me, bent over, gasping for air.

"Oliver?" I asked, trying to make out his face in the dim light.

"Yes, Mr White," he managed to reply between breaths. "I came to receive you."

"Good that you came," I said, relieved.

Oliver was twenty-one, of medium height, and thin. After my broker put up posters around town looking for a helper, he was the first to call me for the job. I hired him immediately, and tonight was the first time we met face-to-face.

"Give me the suitcase. I'll carry it for you. It's a long walk and you all look exhausted. Let me help." Oliver offered, his voice kind but firm. "Here, this is yours now." He placed the keys in my hand and grabbed the luggage."

We started walking. The road stretched on, quiet and dim, and halfway through, I realised how far ahead I had wandered. I stopped and looked back. Leslie, Liam, and Ebba were trailing about 500 meters behind me, their faint outlines barely visible in the foggy distance. Oliver was right at the back, carrying most of the luggage while keeping a watchful eye on them, making sure no one strayed or got lost in the dark.

The streetlights were scattered, one every 50 meters, their weak glow barely cutting through the thick mist. The moon above shone brighter than any of them, though its light struggled to pierce the heavy fog hanging in the air. Beyond a few meters, the world was swallowed by gloom, and the sound of our footsteps was the only thing that filled the silence.

In my excitement, I ignored everything else and quickened my pace. Before I knew it, the house of my dreams stood in front of me—grand, commanding, and almost hypnotic. For a moment, I felt rooted to the spot, unable to look away. A sensation washed over me, as though I'd been here before, though I knew that wasn't possible. I don't know why, but I felt a strange pull toward that house, an unshakable affection that defies reason.

The house was a double-storey structure, held up by two tall pillars. Four arched windows stared back at me from the upper floor, and two more sat on the ground level. Between them, a massive wooden door loomed, weathered yet majestic. Parts of the outer walls had lost their plaster, revealing the raw brick beneath, which only added to its strange haunting beauty. The entire property was surrounded by wild turf that stretched like a carpet under the moonlight.

I stood there, frozen, my heart thudding in my chest. I couldn't move. My legs refused to listen, as if my body and mind were no longer in sync. I was overwhelmed by a feeling I couldn't explain—an intoxicating blend of awe and accomplishment.

This was more than just a house. It was my victory. My proof to the world that Aston White was no ordinary man. I had conquered. I had arrived. For a fleeting second, I felt like a king standing at the gates of his kingdom.

I pushed the iron gate and stepped onto the property. I walked across the pathway to the wooden door and took out the keys, trying to unlock the door. My hands shook, my grip fragile. I couldn't figure out why I felt so nervous—maybe it was the gravity of the moment, the doorway to my new life, the life I had dreamed of for so long. Taking a deep breath, I steadied myself and turned the key.

With a metallic click, the lock surrendered, and the heavy door groaned open into the darkness beyond.

With a slow, creaking groan, the door swung inward at my gentle push. The sound echoed through the emptiness like a whisper of something long forgotten. To my surprise, the lights were already on.

The massive hall stretched before me, coated in layers of dust. Cobwebs hung from the corners like forgotten curtains, swaying slightly in the faint draft. An odd smell filled the air—stale, damp, and tinged with decay—as though the house had been left untouched for decades.

To my right, two doors were shut tight, their wood cracked with age. In the centre of the hall stood a long dining table surrounded by six broken chairs, all of them overturned and sprawled across the floor as if abandoned in a hurry. Beyond the table was the kitchen, shadowed and silent.

Then, from the corner of my eye, something flickered—flames. My heart skipped. I turned sharply to the left, my gaze locking onto a fireplace where wood burned bright and steady. The fire crackled, alive. But there was no warmth, no glow spreading beyond it. In front of the flames, two outdated sofas sat covered in a fine layer of ash.

Beside the fireplace, a staircase rose into darkness. At its end stood a pendulum clock, its face blank, its hands frozen. Not a tick, not a sound. Just silence.

I realised I was still standing at the threshold, my

breath shallow. Forcing myself forward, I stepped inside with a single thought repeating in my mind: Who's going to clean up this mess and make this place livable? I couldn't help but picture Leslie's face.

"What are you doing in the dark? The switchboard is right next to the door. I guess you didn't see it—let me turn it on for you," Oliver said softly from behind me.

I turned around to see Leslie and the kids stepping in with him. But something made me turn back almost instantly to face the hall again. My heart sank. It was pitch dark now—no light, no glow. How was that possible? Just moments ago, everything was visible, bathed in a strange brightness. Now, I couldn't see past a few feet in front of me.

Oliver flipped the switch, and the room lit up. Relief should've washed over me, but what I saw left me frozen. Everything was exactly as I had seen before—the fireplace, the dinner table, the couches. But now it was... spotless. Not a speck of dust or ash in sight. The six chairs were upright and perfectly in place. The fireplace stood cold and unlit, no burning wood, no flickering flames.

Everything seemed unnervingly perfect, except for one thing. The clock at the top of the staircase. It still wasn't ticking.

I stared at it, questions swirling in my mind. Was I hallucinating? Or am I so exhausted that my brain is not getting enough oxygen and playing tricks on me?

I didn't know the answer, but I could feel the discomfort settling deep inside me.

Oliver spoke calmly, "Mr White, I've arranged everything for you. The house is cleaned, and I've prepared dinner. You all must be tired and hungry—go freshen up, and I'll serve the meal. There are three rooms upstairs. Your bedroom is on the left, next to a study room. The kids' room is on the right. Down here, there are two rooms—a smaller one for me and another for guests."

Leslie took in the surroundings, her gaze sweeping every corner of the house. There was no trace of exhaustion on her face. Instead, her eyes lit up with wonder and delight, as though she saw something no one else could. She came over to me, her smile wide and unshaken, and took my hand.

"Thank you for this," she said softly, her voice full of warmth. "This is the best thing anyone could have done. This will be our Happy Place."

Her words were like balm to my distress, but only for a moment. I smiled back, nodding, though my mind was elsewhere.

I had chosen not to tell her the truth—and seeing her this happy, I almost felt justified. Almost.

While my family started exploring, making this place

their own, I stood still. I couldn't shake the questions spinning in my head, couldn't ignore the things I had seen—or thought I'd seen.

What was real?

The fireplace. The dust. The dark, creeping strangeness.

I watched my family laugh and settle in, but inside, the worry gnawed at me. Something didn't feel right.

Could this be the start of something hidden?

CHAPTER TWO

Be My Guest

19th November, 1996

It was our first morning in the house, and we were still trying to settle in. Everything feels unfamiliar. I kept pushing last night's events out of my mind—I couldn't afford to lose focus, not now. Kids needed my support - this place felt alien to them, especially Ebba. She wasn't happy about leaving Birmingham, leaving her friends behind. I need to help her adjust, to make her feel like this house can be home. Leslie will need me, too. There's unpacking to do, rooms to set up, spaces to make ours. She'll want this house to look like the one we left behind, to feel familiar.

But even as I think about all of this, a part of me can't shake the feeling that something about this house doesn't want to be changed.

9:30 A.M.

I went to the study room. This part of the house was something my daughter and I both loved. Most of the room was taken up by books, neatly arranged on shelves along the left side. In the far right corner, there was a cosy chair and a desk with an old-fashioned lamp on it. A window in front of the desk gave a clear view of the outside world. One side opened into a lush, endless forest, while the other was scarred by two small, crumbling houses—old and unsightly, like remnants of a forgotten past. They were the only thing out of place.

I turned back to the books, running my fingers over the hundreds of titles. This treasure was mine now. A strange sense of excitement bubbled up, and then one book caught my eye. **The Invitation**. The title alone sent a strange shiver down my spine. I pulled it free from the shelf, curiosity tightening its grip on me. The leather cover was cracked and brittle, its spine barely holding together. The pages—yellowed, stained, and fragile—felt ancient beneath my fingers, as if they had been waiting too long for someone to turn them. Without a second thought, I opened it and began reading the first page. What I found was unsettling and weird.

The Boundary Fades- Summon them from the Darkness.

Speak the words, light the flame.
The shadowed ones stir, waiting for the call.
Dare to open the gate, and they shall cross.

Your body is theirs.
In your own flesh, you're just a visitor, a stranger. A guest.
Send The Invitation.
Let Them In.

It Is Time.

"Dad, you're here. I've been looking everywhere for you."

Ebba stepped into the room, a cup of tea trembling slightly in her hands.

"Put it on the table," I muttered, barely glancing up. One more page. Just one. Something about this book refused to let me go.

She set the cup down, but her gaze didn't waver from the book in my hands.

"The Invitation," she murmured, reading the title aloud.

I snapped the book shut, forcing myself to pull away, and slid it back to its place—out of reach, out of sight.

"Did you have breakfast?" I asked, trying to steer the conversation elsewhere.

Ebba ignored the question at first, her eyes still locked on where the book had been.

"Ebba?" I said, sharper this time.

She blinked, snapping out of it. "Breakfast? Yes. Oliver made coffee, and Mom gave me toast."

"Sounds like you had a good morning."

"You could say that," she replied, her voice quieter now. "But today's going to be long. Liam and I unloaded the items, and Oliver and Mom are doing their best to embellish every corner. But it's not enough." She looked straight at me. "We need you, Dad."

I looked at her, hearing the words but sensing something deeper—the significance they carried. She was just a child, but there was a calm authority in her voice that didn't belong to someone her age.

"You go, I'll follow," I said.

She paused, eyeing me suspiciously. "Are you sure?"

I smiled and nodded, reassuring her.

Without another word, she turned and hurried downstairs, not wasting a second.

Stood there for a moment longer. I don't like being told what to do, but with her—well, it's different. There are only two women in my life who can get away with it.

I picked up the cup of tea, knowing I'd better move now. Staying put wouldn't end well for me.

1:30 P.M.

"Mr White, you called me?" Oliver asked as he walked into the bedroom.

"Ah, there you are. Where were you?"

"I went to the market to get some veggies for tonight," he explained.

"Alright, listen. I need you to go to the post office right now and dispatch this letter. It must be done before 5 o'clock. And one more thing—now that I think of it—the clock on the staircase is out of order. See if you can fix it when you're back."

"Will be done," Oliver replied.

I turned away to rearrange my bed, but something felt off. I didn't hear any footsteps leaving the room.

When I looked back, Oliver was still there, standing still as a statue, staring at me.
"What?" I asked, a little sharper this time.

"Anything else, Mr White?" he asked politely.

"No, you can leave," I said.

"Okay." he acknowledged and finally walked out of the room.

"That letter is for your publisher, or do you have another woman in your life you're hiding from me?" Leslie teased, shutting the wardrobe after tidying up the clothes.
With my head down and a smirk on my face, I replied, "You caught me."

We both laughed and headed downstairs for lunch. The kids were already seated at the table, waiting with looks of pure desperation.

"Come fast, please! I'm starving to death," Ebba groaned dramatically.

"Just two more minutes, I swear!" Leslie's voice drifted from the kitchen, light yet hurried. "The meal is almost ready.

"What's on the menu today?" I asked, trying to sound hopeful.

From the kitchen, Leslie answered casually, "Didn't

have many options, so it's very basic—veg sandwiches, carrot soup, and eggs."
There was a pause. Liam glanced at Ebba. Ebba glanced at me. I looked back at both of them. Without saying a single word, the three of us shared a moment of silent despair. The disappointment in the room was so thick you could spread it on toast—if we'd had any better options.

Leslie emerged from the kitchen with the 'meal' and set it on the table, her expression wary. Clearly, she noticed the collective gloom on our faces.

"It's been a hectic day," she explained, a little too quickly. "I didn't have time, and I was too tired to make anything better. But don't worry—Oliver's brought groceries, so dinner will be decent."

"Thank you, Mom, for the lunch," Ebba said graciously, probably sensing Leslie's exhaustion. "It's fine, we understand."

Leslie visibly relaxed, relieved by the response, and sat down to join us.

Meanwhile, I poked at my sandwich and whispered to Liam, "At least dinner will save us."

Liam muttered back with a cheerful look, "If we survive till then."

5:00 P.M.

I stepped outside with Liam, wanting to get a feel for the place and maybe build some connections with the neighbourhood. I'd asked the ladies to come along, but Leslie was taking a well-deserved rest after carrying most of the day's load, and Ebba was busy exploring the study room.

The day was winding down. The sun dipped lower on the horizon, and the air grew cooler. Holding Liam's hand, I pushed open the heavy iron gate, its creak cutting through the quiet. We stepped out.

To our right, a wall of dense timberland loomed, the trees tangled together in an unsettling way, hiding whatever lay beyond. To the left, two small houses stood side by side, their exteriors cracked and crumbling. They looked abandoned—silent and forgotten.

Curiosity got the better of me, so we walked toward them. I let go of Liam's hand and knocked on the door of the first house. The sound echoed faintly, and we waited. Nothing. No footsteps, no voices—just the wind shifting through the trees.

We moved to the second house, smaller and more broken down than the first. I knocked again, harder this time. The silence felt heavier here, like the house itself was holding its breath. No one answered.

Liam looked up at me. "No one lives here, Daddy?"

I shook my head. "I don't think so."

"But why?" he asked, his voice small.
I grinned to lighten the mood. "Maybe our house is bigger than theirs, and they couldn't handle the jealousy. So they packed up and left forever."

Liam nodded, satisfied by the explanation, and let go of my hand to play near the gate. His tiny figure seemed so out of place in the eerie quiet.

"Let's go, Liam," I called after a moment. "We need to help mommy with dinner. And remember, we have to visit your school tomorrow for the formalities. You need to sleep early, right?"
"Coming, Daddy! Just two minutes!" he shouted, his voice the only sound in the stillness.

As I stood there waiting, my gaze drifted toward the woods. The smog was thickening, blurring the trees and making it harder to see beyond them. Still, there was something captivating about it—it complemented the house, enhancing its charm, like a scene from an old painting.

"Let's go, Daddy," Liam whispered, tugging at my hand. His voice was quieter than before, almost as if he, too, sensed something watching from the trees.

I grabbed his hand and walked towards the gate. Just as we reached it, I looked once more toward the forest, admiring its calm. But this time, my heart skipped a beat. Behind the trees, half-hidden in the mist, I saw someone—motionless, staring straight at me.

An icy shiver ran down my spine. For a moment, I considered going closer to see who or what it was. But Liam was with me, and the thought of wild animals lurking nearby made me hesitate. Better not to risk it.

"Liam, go inside," I hissed.
He looked up at me with intrigue but obeyed, dashing toward the house. As soon as he disappeared behind the door, I turned back to the forest, stepped forward cautiously, telling myself that if it's an animal, I'd keep my distance. But what if it wasn't? What if someone needed help?

I had barely taken a few steps when I realised the figure was gone. The spot where it had been was now empty, swallowed by the smog. Still, I pushed on, hoping to find some trace of whoever or whatever I had seen. I searched the ground, scanned the trees, but there was nothing.

I sighed and turned to head back. That's when I heard it—a sharp crunch. The sound of a dry leaf cracking underfoot. I froze. Slowly, I spun around.

And there she was.

An old woman stood behind the nearest tree, as if trying to hide. Her hands clung to the bark, and her body shook slightly, as if she had seen something horrifying. Her face was lined with light wrinkles, her skin pale and worn. Strands of grey hair framed her face in a tangled mess. Her mouth was partially open, revealing brown, decaying teeth, as if she'd been chewing on dirt. She wore an old, tattered gown, faded and filthy, torn in several places, hanging off her frail frame.

For a long moment, we stared at each other in silence. Her eyes were wide with fear, as though I was the thing to be afraid of.

"Who are you, and what are you doing here at this time of day?" I asked, keeping my voice calm, careful not to startle her further.
The old woman didn't respond. Her wide, anxious eyes flicked toward me, as if deciding whether to trust me or run away.

"Hello? Can you hear me?" I tried again. She still said nothing. I took a small step closer, but she flinched, so I stopped where I was.

"You want help? You can tell me. I will not harm you."

Her voice finally broke the silence, shaky but clear. "Are you the tenant of that house?"

The question caught me off guard, and I let out a short, dry chuckle. She stared at me, unblinking.

"No, no. I'm actually the owner," I replied, trying to

ease the tension.

At that, she stepped out from behind the tree and faced me. Her hunched frame straightened just enough to surprise me. She tilted her head with a curt smile. "Then it's you who should be afraid, not me," she said, her tone sharp.

Before I could respond, she walked past me with confidence that didn't match her dull appearance.

"What do you mean?" I called after her, quickly turning to follow. "Hello, I'm talking to you!"

She stopped and turned, her expression colder now. "Do you know what happened in that house?"

I paused for a moment, choosing my words carefully. "The killings?"

Her lips tightened. "So you do know and you still decided to come here?" There was disbelief in her voice, almost as though she was accusing me of something.

"So what?" I shrugged. "People die. That shouldn't stop us from living. What happened there was tragic, yes, but I'm grateful for it. If it weren't for those events, I wouldn't have got that beautiful house at such a bargain. Now I own it, and I have no regrets."

The old woman's face fell. Her disappointment was palpable, as though she'd hoped for a different kind

of person to stand before her. She gave me a long, icy stare before muttering, "You have no idea what's headed your way."
As I tried to make sense of her words, she added, "Did you find any book?" Before I could answer, she continued, "A word of advice—don't read it."

Without a word, she turned and walked away; her steps were slow and deliberate, leaving a chill in the air that lingered long after she was gone.

I stepped closer to the gate, trying to make sense of everything and thought to myself—if everyone continues to act strange, Leslie would get suspicious. That's the last thing I need now. I pushed open the iron gate, but before going inside, I glanced back at her. She was walking toward the second abandoned house, the one next door.

It hit me like a punch to the gut—she lives there. I smacked my forehead in realization. How lucky I was to have such... interesting neighbours.

5:45 P.M.

Oliver was back, sitting on the stairs, working on the old clock.

I walked over. "Did you post the letter?"

He looked up and stood. "Yes, Mr White. It's done. Here's the receipt." He paused, then added, "I noticed how curious you were about it. What did it say?" I narrowed my eyes. "Do your job, Oliver. Don't be nosy."

It had barely been 24 hours since we met, and already he was asking questions that weren't his business. You had to set boundaries right from the start—otherwise, people like him would start poking into your private life.

"Sorry, Mr. White. I shouldn't have asked," he mumbled, looking down.

Leslie, sitting at the dinner table chopping veggies, noticed the sudden shift in my behaviour and Oliver's mood. She could never stand seeing anyone upset.

"Yes, Oliver, it was important," she chimed in, offering a kind grin to ease the discomfort. "He sent the letter to his media company, letting them know about our new home so he can keep working from here."

"Oh! Then it was very important," Oliver replied, looking relieved.

They exchanged polite smiles, and I stood there, feeling like a fool. Leslie was being kind, but sharing details like that wasn't always a good idea. Oliver was still a stranger, and she shouldn't be spilling our private information so easily.

The two of them went back to their tasks, and I

asked, "Where's Ebba?"

Leslie responded sharply, not even glancing at me. Her voice carried a hint of anger. "Upstairs, in the study room."

I could tell she didn't like the way I'd spoken to Oliver. I didn't press the matter further. Without another word, I left the hall and made my way upstairs to the study.

Ebba was sitting in the chair, the table positioned nearly in front of her. A thick book in her hands, the table lamp casting a soft glow over her face.

"Ebba, have you finished prepping? We're going to your new school tomorrow," I asked.

"I'll take care of it soon," she murmured, still lost in her book.

"This book can wait. It's not going anywhere. First, get up and do what's needed."

With an exasperated sigh, she set the book down, shot me an annoyed look, and left the room without a word.

I muttered under my breath, "The apple doesn't fall far from the tree. She's just like her mother."

It was the same book I had been reading in the morning. Gently, I placed it back on the table, turned off the lamp, and moved the armchair in front of the window. Closing the pane to block out the chill, I sank into the chair, letting the quiet of the room to settle around me. Darkness enveloped the space, broken only by the soft glow of the moonlight streaming through the window.

I knew I needed to start working on my articles. My leaves were almost over—but for the moment, I let my eyelids fall shut. I chose to do nothing and enjoy the stillness of the present.

Time slipped away, and Leslie's voice woke me up. "You're sleeping?"

I jolted upright, heart racing. "What time is it?"

"10:30. Come on, dinner's ready, and it's getting cold. Better put on your jacket."

The day's exhaustion had left me drained, my body begging for rest. I stood and followed her as she exited the room. I pushed the chair back into place, adjusting it to match the room's layout. Moving toward the window, I reached to draw the curtains, but noticed something odd. The glass was covered in fog, yet there were marks on it, as if someone had traced something with a finger.

I stepped closer, squinting to read what it said. The message only deepened my confusion, a chill creeping through me. I read it aloud, my voice shaking: *Welcome Mr. White, be my guest.*

The words had been written moments ago; I was sure of it. But as I stared, the fog began to creep back, slowly erasing the message as if it had never been there.

I bolted from the room and spotted Leslie in the hallway, heading for the stairs. My voice cracked as I called out, "Did you write something on the window when you came to wake me?"

She turned, raising an eyebrow. "No, why? What's going on?"

"Nothing," I muttered. How could I explain this confusion? What did I even say in response?

She continued downstairs, and I returned to the room. The message had completely vanished, swallowed by the fog.

I stayed rooted to the spot, utterly confused, as a sudden wave of dizziness swept over me. Clutching the table for balance, my brows furrowed—the book was gone.

"I left it right here. Where did it go?" muttered to himself. "Ebba... it must be her. She probably took it and pulled this prank on me."

A faint chuckle escaped my lips. Out of nowhere, Leslie's voice rang out, crisp and distinct. Called from downstairs, dragging me back to the present.

CHAPTER THREE

Chanting

15th December, 1996
11:00 P.M.

Christmas is approaching. Only 10 days away, we prepare to celebrate our first holiday in this new house, filling it with warmth and the promise of many more cherished memories to come. From tomorrow, Ebba and Liam will enjoy their holiday, but Leslie and I will continue to work for a few more days, keeping the rhythm of our routines before fully embracing the festival break.

Like every year I find myself missing you both so much and writing this letter, wishing you were here to celebrate with us. I love you, mom and dad and hope you are at peace.
Your son,
Aston.

Wiped away my tears and rested my head on the couch, gazing up at the ceiling. The fire, now just embers in the fireplace, still kept me warm.

"Since college, I've written a letter to my parents every year, always hoping—maybe foolishly—that one day, I'd hand it to them myself... on the other side. It's been two decades now, but it feels like yesterday that I lost my mom. We lived in a tiny one-room house, with my dad mostly away for work. We struggled financially. I even resorted to stealing food from the neighbours at times. One day, my dad walked out on us and never returned. Mom waited. Days turned into months, then years, but he never returned. People say he found someone else, someone he thought was better than my mom. Which I refused to believe. As time passed, I came to terms with the fact that he was gone, but mom clung to hope, unable to accept the reality. I watched her cry every night until her body simply couldn't take it anymore and she fell ill. We had no money for treatment. One night, she went to sleep and never woke up. It was unbearably hard to accept, but there was no other choice. That same year I got into a college and that's when this ritual of writing letters began."

"I'm sorry for what you've been through, Mr. White," Oliver said, his voice softer than usual. "Sounds like you've come a long way." Oliver said this with a consoling grin on his face. He continued, "would you like me to make you another drink?"

I covered my glass and said no.

Oliver said- "I'm glad you shared this with me."

"I am glad that you listened. Go to sleep now. It's getting late." I said.

"Okay, but feel free to call me if you need anything. Good night"

"Good night." I replied

He then went into his room and shut the door.

In the past few days, our bond has depended, and I found that I have begun to trust him more.

I sat by the window, watching the last embers flicker in the fireplace, their glow fading into shadows. The warmth lingered, but it did little to chase away the chill settling in my chest. I was about to get up and head to the bedroom when the clock on the wall at the top of the staircase stuck at midnight. Its chime echoed through the room like a church. This happens every night, and I loathe the sound of that bell.

I finished my last peg and went to the kitchen. As I placed the empty glass on the counter, a faint creak from above caught my attention. The sound was soft, deliberate footsteps of someone moving on the floor above me. I slowly moved towards the stairs to catch another hint of movement, but the house had fallen silent again. I scanned, but everything seemed untouched and there was no one.

Quickly, I ascended the stairs. My pulse quickened

as I reached the top. The dim hallway light barely reached the top of the staircase, casting long, shifting shadows along the floor. I first made my way to my bedroom, where Leslie was deep in sleep. I exhaled a deep, shaky breath, a fleeting movement of relief. Then, leaving Leslie undisturbed, I moved towards the kid's room. Liam was tucked under his blanket, but Ebba's bed was empty. The bathroom door was ajar.

"Ebba? Are you there?" I said, but there was no reply. I moved ahead and peered inside with hesitation, and there was no one. A rare chill of fear gripped me. I realised if she is not here, then only one place is left, the study room.

"She must be buried in her books again. Should have checked the time at least, just because her holidays had started didn't mean she could abandon her routine." I headed to the study room, determined to bring her back to her bed.

As I stepped into the room, the emptiness consumed me. A lone candle flickered weakly on the floor, but its feeble glow swallowed by the surrounding darkness. In its faint circle of light, a shadowy figure sat motionless, their back to me. I could hear a faint, creepy murmur- a voice, but not one I recognised. It was high and thin, resembling that of an elderly woman. My heart pounded as I stumbled, finding the switch. With a sudden flick, the lights blazed to life, spreading a faint glow throughout the room. There, on the floor, Ebba knelt—her back unnaturally arched, her head tilted toward the ceiling. Her lips moved, but the voice that escaped them was not her own.

"Ebba!" I screamed, the sound tearing from my throat.

Her head snapped towards me, eyes wide and hollow. The moment our gazes locked, she slumped to the floor over the candle, her body collapsing in a faint. The room was quiet now, but there was a heaviness in the air.

I took her to her room in my arms, placed her back in bed and spent the entire night awake watching over, fearing she might start sleepwalking again. It's something she has never done before, or perhaps something I have never noticed.

Was this just exhaustion? A nightmare? Or was something far worse at play?

8:00 A.M.

My eyes are weary. The events of last night kept flashing before me, which kept me awake. I need to find a way to help my daughter.

The children were asleep while Leslie was already up and dressed, ready for work.

"I am coming with you." I said.
"To the hospital?" Leslie replied in shock.

"Yes, actually it's been almost a month and I haven't ventured out anywhere. This town still feels new to me. Today I am taking a break from work and would love to join you."

How could I explain what I had seen yesterday? The eerie chanting, the way Ebba collapsed... I couldn't make sense of it myself. Maybe it was better to say nothing at all.

Leslie- "Go get ready then. I am already getting late."

She was happy that I was joining her, but beneath my calm exterior, I had a purpose- to uncover the truth behind everything that has happened to me and Ebba.

9:15 A.M.

We stepped off the bus and headed towards the hospital. It was a vast, imposing building painted white with an array of endless windows on all its three floors. The hospital name was emblazoned in bold red letters, standing out prominently from afar. A steady flow of people moved in and out of the hospital doors, their faces a mix of exhaustion and urgency. The building itself loomed, sterile and unyielding, under the grey morning sky.

"I work on the 2nd floor in the behavioural health ward. Would you like to take a look?"
"Why not? I would love to."

I replied, and she curved her lips and continued forward, gesturing to me to follow her.

The ground and first floor were bustling with noise and crowd, but the second floor was a stark contrast. Here, only a few nurses and administrative staff were visible and an utter quietness pervaded the space.

"Has someone passed away here? Why does this floor feel so distinct from the others?" I inquired softly. Pressing my hand to my mouth as if to shield my curiosity from the silence.

"It's because of that." Leslie lifted her eyebrows and subtly arched them towards a board- **Mental Health Ward:***please be silent.*

"We have over 40 patients here," she continued, "And any sudden noise or overcrowding can easily trigger their anxiety or panic attacks, turning them aggressive." She explained in a low and cautious voice, as if afraid of disturbing the fragile calm.

As we walked down the corridor, a slim, tall lady approached from the opposite direction, raising her hand in a wave towards Leslie. Leslie returned the gesture. With long, purposeful strides, the lady drew closer. She clutched a stack of files in one hand while with the other; tucked a stray strand of her hair behind her ear. Her movements were effortless. She wore a crisp white lab coat, a badge pinned to the front bearing her name—Dr Alice Robinson.

"Doctor?" I said to myself in shock. "She looks like a college going girl."

Dr. Alice approached with an easy confidence, offering Leslie a warm smile. "Good morning."

"Good morning, doctor." Leslie replied.

"You are late today." Dr Alice remarked with concern.

"Meet my husband, Mr Aston White," Leslie introduced me with a hint of light-hearted frustration. "He decided on a whim to join me today and you know how men are, they take forever to get ready but never admit it and blame us instead." As she spoke, they both exchanged amused glances. Feeling a sudden wave of awkwardness, I offered a nervous, uncertain smile in response.

"Oh! So he is the one who bought that mansion for you? It's a pleasure to meet you, Mr White." Dr Alice extended her hand.

I immediately liked the vibe of this lady, maybe because she was the only one who had not reacted weirdly upon learning about my house, and that was a relief. "Likewise" I also stretched my arm, and we shook hands.

"She is from Manchester and has recently arrived here to practise neurology." Leslie explained.

A neurologist. She could answer my questions, unravel the doubts that baffled me. This suffocating state of confusion is closing in on me and I just hope that she is the one to rescue me from its grip.

"Give me five minutes to change and I will join you guys," Leslie said

"Could you please take these files and hold on to them for me? I will retrieve them later." Dr Alice requested.

"Sure, why not?" Leslie replied.

She handed the pile of files over, and with a nod of acknowledgement, Leslie turned and left.

Dr Alice then looked at me and said, "Actually, my hand started to ache. Those were too heavy."

"I understand," replied with a steady voice as I absorbed the not so important information.

We both began to walk side by side, making our way towards the end of the corridor.

"How is the new place coming along for you?" I asked to cut the awkwardness.

"It's a charming small town to be honest, offering all the amenities and filled with warm, welcoming people. I am really enjoying it here." Dr Alice replied and asked, "What about you? Relocating to an entirely new place is never easy."

I nodded in agreement. "At first, I was nervous about how everything would unfold, but Leslie's support made all the difference. She made it possible." We shared a grin and kept marching forward.
I had so much to ask, but where do I ever begin? Will I make any sense to her or she will think I am going paranoid?

"What is bothering you? Can share if you want to." Dr Alice fixed her gaze on me.

"Not quite sure how to put this into words," I answered

She came to a halt and turned to face me. "You can at least give it a try."

I took a deep breath, knowing it was time to recount everything that had happened since the very first day in that house, hoping to receive a reasonable explanation from her that could make sense of those events. I began to reveal everything, and as I spoke, she listened intently, her eyes locked onto mine with a focused, tense quiet. Her expression remained unreadable, but I could tell she was absorbing every detail. She nodded occasionally, as if piecing together a puzzle, while her fingers curled slightly against the armrest.
"I'm grateful you felt comfortable enough to express yourself and confide in me." Dr Alice voiced her

words with steadiness.
"I feel lighter now that I have spoken, and there is just one request. Please don't mention any of this to Leslie, she knows nothing about it."

"Don't worry, I will not."

"So, what's your take on all this? Is there any reasoning for what is happening?" I asked.

Pausing briefly, she replied, "You know, when we become too eager for something, we begin to live that moment before it actually arrives. In your case, it was that house you so desperately wanted to inhabit and call your own. Correct me if I am wrong. Before you even set foot inside, your subconscious likely conjured all sorts of scenarios, from the worst to the best.

What you experienced when you first entered might have been nothing more than your mind playing tricks on you, showing you what you didn't want to see. There is a possibility that something triggered a deep-seated childhood trauma, but more than that, I believe the intense combination of exhaustion and excitement causes your perception to wrap.

And what happened with Ebba is actually quite common. Sleepwalking can result from various factors like inconsistent bedtimes, unfamiliar or uncomfortable environments, or insufficient sleep. What we should notice is that she went to that particular room even though she could have wandered anywhere. It could be an overstimulation. Books comfort her, so even in her sleep she sought them out for a sense of tranquillity. The only thing I'm uncertain about is that candle. Why did she have it? But apart from that, everything else seems fine. There is nothing to worry about, Mr White. You and Ebba are both perfectly normal."

She smiled softly and I let out a sigh of relief, feeling my heart return to its normal rhythm.

"You have no idea how relieved I am now. Thank you."

She acknowledged my gratitude with a gentle flutter of her eyelashes.

"Relieved, from what? What were you both talking about?" Leslie asked with a look of confusion and her eyebrows raised. She stood behind us, utterly clueless about the conversation. Before I had the chance to explain, Dr. Alice interjected "It's nothing serious. He was just concerned about your shift timings during Christmas. I assured him I would make sure you get time off around then, so you can spend the festival with your family."

Before anyone could say another word, a nurse came rushing towards Dr Alice, whispering something urgently in her ear. I watched her expression shifting, tension tightening her features. She glanced at Leslie, giving a quick, subtle nod. Leslie mirrored the gesture and straight after that, Dr Alice hurried away, leaving an uneasy silence behind.

"What just happened?" I asked in confusion.

Leslie shot me a nervous glance and said, "Follow me." her face was carved with concern. I could sense something was wrong.

She moved swiftly. Every step she took was filled with urgency, and I struggled to keep up. As we navigated the corridor, she finally spoke. Her voice was low, but serious. "We have a very special patient here. He is kept isolated on the third floor, away from everyone else."

"But why?" I asked.

"Shh..." she placed a finger on her lips and signalled me to lower my voice.

We ascended to the third floor, where the lights were subdued, casting spooky shadows across the corridor. At the end of the hall stood a solitary room, from a muffled, desperate screen through the heavy door. Leslie's voice cut through the tension. "His name is Gerald," she explained in a hushed tone, her eyes wary. "He has been here since childhood. They say he becomes particularly volatile at this time of the year. In the past, he has attacked a few nurses and tried to choke them. Controlling him now is a struggle. It takes hours and even medication has lost its effect."

As we approached the door, the distant scream grew

louder, amplifying the chilling reality of the situation.

"Is it possible for me to see him, even from a distance?" I asked and made sure to keep my voice low this time.

Leslie took a moment, then nodded reluctantly. We approached the hefty door with its small glass window at the top. Peering inside, through that small, reinforced glass, I saw Dr Alice giving an injection to a middle-aged man. Both of his arms were shackled and his right leg was also restrained. He was sprawled in agony. Suddenly, he noticed me watching and fell numb. Slowly, he lifted his head, fixing me with an unblinking stare. Then he propped himself up and sat on the bed in a straight posture, still not breaking the eye contact with me.

Is he aware of who I am?

After a few minutes, Dr Alice emerged from the room with three nurses in tow. They appeared relaxed, as if they had conquered a formidable form. And she murmured softly, "We should leave now."

Before departing, I decided to take one last glance inside the room. I let the others move ahead, slipping quietly to the door when their attention was elsewhere. Peering in, what I saw next gave me a cold shiver. My mouth fell open, and eyes widened in terror.

Gerald was sitting on his knees, mimicking Ebba's

posture from the previous night. He was chanting the same worrisome mantra she had uttered in the same rhythm, word by word.

The days are drowned beneath the murky sky,
And nights are choked with fear.

This place is nothing but a pit of dark,
A lair where none should dare.

If you've come, you've sealed your fate,
Your end lurks near.

There's no way out, they'll drag you into the fire,
Your soul is bound to them forever here.

I felt a hand on my shoulder and twirled around, my heart hammering.

"Let's go," said Dr Alice, her voice tight with worry.

"He's... he's reciting some spell," I buzzed, my voice wobbling.

Her expression obscured her silence, telling more than words. "You know what it is, don't you?" I asked, pressing for an answer.

Dr. Alice hesitated, her lips parting as if to speak—but then she stopped. A shadow crossed her face. When she finally spoke, her voice was barely above a whisper. "All I know is... it's bad. Something cursed."

CHAPTER FOUR

Twenty Years Ago

22nd December, 1996
11:30 A.M.

"Daddy, Christmas is only three days away! Why don't you seem excited? You've been acting different these past few days." Liam asked with purity.

"I am excited, son. Why did you think that way?" I tried to be normal.

"I can tell. You haven't helped me with my homework, and you don't even give me goodnight kisses anymore." Whenever this happens, it usually means something is bothering you," he replied and stood before me, gently placing his tiny palm on my clasped hands and said again, "You can tell me, daddy. I promise I will listen."

His innocent eyes met mine, filled with quiet concern. "There is nothing to worry about, son. With Christmas approaching, there is so much left to do—decorations, shopping and sending holiday cards and gifts to our relatives. Will you help me?"

"Why not daddy? I will take care of the decorations. You go shopping because I don't have any money." He pulled out his empty pocket as proof, and we both laughed.

"Wait, I am coming." He said and went out of the room running and then came back in a blink "Here," he said, handing me his tape recorder. "Whenever you feel sad or alone, just talk into it. It'll be our little secret. Or you can also think that you're talking to me. You'll feel good afterwards." I smiled and took that from him. "This is my Christmas gift to you, daddy"

After hearing this, it was hard for me to stay low. I scooped him up into my arms and kissed his fluffy, soft cheeks with affection.

Leslie entered the bedroom with messy hair, flour smeared across her cheek and wearing a well-worn apron. And said, "Oliver is putting string lights outside and Ebba is helping him. You should set off now for the shopping trip; the list is long and will probably consume the entire day."

Liam raised his hand and said, "I will decorate the hall."

"Alright, both, let's get to work." she departed the moment she had assigned us the tasks.
"Okay, I have to go now. I have got stuff to do. Please put me down, daddy."

"I love you, son." kissed him again and allowed him to go.

Before he left the room, he turned back and replied, "I love you, too."

For the first time since the hospital, the weight on my chest lifted—even if just for a moment. I quickly prepared myself and set out for the market.

7:00 P.M.

Leslie was right; the shopping absorbed my entire day and energy. Night had fallen, and the moon hid behind a thick shroud of brooding clouds. A restless wind howled through the trees, carrying the scent of damp earth and something... else. The void consumed everything. Yet from a distance, my house illuminated, casting a festive glow that made it look like a celebration.

Stepping off the bus, I approached the rusted iron gate. My eyes drifted toward the old woman's house—a stark contrast to mine. My home shimmered with twinkling lights, alive with warmth. Hers sat in darkness, save for two flickering candles on the doorstep, their flames trembling in the wind, as if resisting the night itself.

A few drops splashed against my face—a sign of the coming rain, carried by the rising wind. Right before my eyes, those fluttering candles got snuffed out. It also erased the old lady's modest effort to beautify her abode. My head dropped, and I stood there for a moment, bathed in the light cascade of water droplets. I altered my path and decided to visit her instead.

I stood before her door and knocked twice. In an instant, I heard, "Who's there?" and I quickly replied, "It's me, your neighbour."

Old lady- "Give me a minute."

The rain grew heavier, and I struggled to protect the shopping bags from becoming drenched. Just then, I heard a faint click as the door unlocked from inside.

The lady stood before me, draped in another worn, faded gown, just like the previous time. I couldn't help but wonder to myself- why does she live like this?

"Hello ma'am, may I come in? Or I will get wet out here." I pleaded

"Why are you here?" she asked, her voice sharp, her frail body planted firmly in the doorway—like a soldier guarding a forbidden border.

"Christmas is coming," I said, forcing a smile. "I thought I'd drop by, you know... since we're neighbors. It's our first holiday in this town, after all." I forced a smile, my fake grin wavering as I regretted stepping out of my cocoon of solitude.

She stepped aside, granting me entry. It was clear she didn't want me there. Her lack of excitement spoke volume.

My bedroom felt larger than this entire house. The bare walls, stripped of plaster, seemed ready to collapse at any moment. She had done her best to clean the floor, but it was a losing battle. The torn curtains were hung, and the atmosphere was thick with the unmistakable stench of decay, like a dead rat hidden somewhere nearby. Gesturing towards the battered couch, she said, "Do you want some water?"

"No, I am good." I didn't want to have anything there; from what I could see, there was no sign of hygiene.

She then sat across from me, one leg casually crossed over the other, exuding an air of ownership over this fragile little house.

"I am here to invite you to my house for Christmas. It will be nice if you can come and meet my wife, Leslie, and our kids."

With no expression, she replied, "I can't. I go to church every year on that day. But thank you for inviting me."

It was glaringly evident that she wasn't keen and was merely offering flimsy excuses.

"I insist," tried to press more. "If you can, then

please come."

"Don't you understand? I can't go there and I would suggest that you leave that place as soon as possible." She said furiously.

"But why?" I asked, confusion mingling and a growing sense of anxiety.

"Because that house is sinful," she whispered, her voice brittle. "It thirsts for blood. "The air now felt heavy with something unspoken.

"What do you mean by that?" I asked, my voice low and quivering. I wanted to reject her words, but deep down, a part of me was craving to hear more. Somewhere inside I had already accepted it, the truth that there is something wrong at my place. I don't know why, but the certainty gnawed at me.We sat in stillness, eyes locked, the weight of unspoken words was felt around us. Then, without warning, she began to speak.

"It was 1975," she said this and a rumble of thunder provided a horrific deafening backdrop to the scene. The night deepened, gloom spreading as the rain intensified, drumming relentlessly against the roof. She gathered her composure and started unravelling the layers of the past.

"I was twenty-six, living with my parents in this house, crushed by financial strain. My father, a schoolteacher, struggled to make ends meet, so I decided to take up a babysitting job for Mr Hawkins' children. He was the owner of that mansion.

Back then, I was just a girl—young, naive, and desperate for work. Babysitting seemed like an easy job. I had no idea it would become the biggest mistake of my life. William Hawkins resided there with his wife, Stella Hawkins, and two children. The household was managed by a single servant reputed to be fiercely loyal to Mr Hawkins, and they also had a cook. She was roughly my age.

As I stepped into their lives, I was introduced to the shadows that loomed over that seemingly ordinary house. The harboured secrets, buried, that they were determined to keep from the world at any cost."

The wind howled, rattling the windows behind me, and just as she was about to speak, the lights flickered out. In an instant, the room was plugged into pitch-black silence.

"Wait, I will get a candle," she said, voice barely cutting through the isolation.

I listened as her footsteps faded and after a few minutes she returned, a dimming candle in her hand dropping just enough light to reveal her face. The wrinkles on her forehead, sagging skin and hollowed eyes made the sight unsettling, almost eerie. If I hadn't known her, I might have fled right then. But how could she be only 47 when she looked as though she had lived a century?

She settled into her chair, wasting no time and dived straight into the story, with a gentle voice, "Mr Hawkins was a well-known builder, both in town and beyond. He had multiple properties to his name, and his wealth made him snobbish. Rumours swirled about his connections with powerful figures. No one in the town ever dared to show him disrespect. It wasn't always because he earned it, but more out of fear. His short temper, rude demeanor, and imposing physique kept people at a distance. A tall, strong personality who always dressed in suits even when he had nowhere to go, he carried himself with a regal air that left an impression on anyone who crossed his path. He was somewhat of your age only at that time.

His father had been in the army - a strict man with a cold heart. He left Mr. Hawkins two things: a gold military signet ring and his aura. He was meticulous to the brink of obsession, and I don't recall ever seeing him laugh. Since then, I have never encountered anyone quite like him. A man of such commanding presence, with an unshakeable image and dominating stature, had only one weakness- his family and that manor.

The terrifying truth was that there were enemies no one knew about, who were lurking nearby, hiding behind friendly faces, waiting patiently for the perfect moment to strike. Mr Hawkins and his family were also unaware of it."

"Who were they, these enemies?" my curiosity made

me impatient.

"Do not interrupt," she said, taking a deep breath to study herself. "You will learn in time. Be patient." Her tone was as firm and unyielding as a headmaster's.

"Okay, sorry," I muttered, recognising my mistake and falling quiet, eager to hear more.

She began, "Most of his time was spent away on business trips, but when Stella got pregnant in 1973, everything changed. She became his priority. He put his work and travel on hold, dedicating himself entirely to be by her side, ensuring her well-being. Beneath his tough exterior, there was a softness reserved only for his wife. When she gave birth to their first child, Arthur, his joy was boundless. He celebrated by hosting an extravagant party at the house, inviting every prominent figure, making the occasion grandeur.

We were their neighbours, yet our names never made it onto the guest list. My parents were disappointed, but I understood our status simply didn't measure up to theirs.

For a couple of months, everything seemed fine, but then things slowly began to take a darker, more complicated turn.

Stella was an attractive lady, but she was the opposite of Mr. Hawkins—warm and kind-hearted, a woman beloved by all. Every Christmas eve, she would bring gifts to our house and after Arthur was born, she came with him to receive my parent's blessings. There was a purity to her that made her impossible not to admire. When I joined as a babysitter, gradually, the bond grew closer during the mornings spent working there from 8 to 11:00 A.M, with those three hours committed to Stella and the baby. In the beginning, conversations flowed easily; she shared her thoughts, sought opinions and went out of the way to make me feel at comfort. But over time, subtle changes crept in. Her once open and friendly nature grew distant and withdrawn, her words fewer and warmth got faded. The devoted mother, who never left her children's side, began to drift away from them. Soon, the once - loving home felt unbalanced, and everything started to spiral out of control. My three hour job quietly stretched into seven, a consequence of her worsening condition.

Mr. Hawkins stepped away from his work and gave all his time to her, while his close friend, Dr. George Hart took over her case, visiting whenever necessary and ensuring he was always nearby.

I had seen Dr. George before at their events; he was around 5 feet 8 inches, impeccably dressed in formal attire, with a well-groomed beard and a signature hat that added to his refined look. In the beginning, his optimism was contagious. He treated Stella but with time, even he began to lose hope.

One evening, I overheard a conversation between

him and Mr Hawkins. They both sat in an uncomfortable quiet on the couch. The crackling fire cast long wavering shapes across the hall, their warmth doing little to thaw the cold tension between them.

"Her condition is worsening by the day," Dr. Hart said, his voice edged with worry. "We need to admit her, or this could go out of control."

Mr Hawkins' response was cold and resolute. "I will turn this house into a hospital before I let her go anywhere. I don't want anyone knowing. There are already enough rumours about my child, and now I don't want them to discuss my wife's condition."

"First of all, he is not your blood. He was found eating his dead mother's flesh since then only people started calling him a Satan's child. And second, people see me visiting daily here, William. You think they don't find that suspicious?" Dr. Hart countered.

"Let them wonder," Dr. Hawkins replied, his jaw clenched. "She is not leaving."

Dr. Hart's voice lowered, filled with warning. "Then I don't think I can help you anymore."

Mr Hawkins looked at him with rage and said, tone obscured, "I'll make her better, with or without you. I will find a better doctor. All you have done is take my money and waste my time. It's been months and there is no sign of improvement in her." He rose to his feet. "You can leave George."

That was the last time Dr. Hart set foot in that house until that fatal night. Time passed, more doctors came and went, each trying in vain. Mr. Hawkins gave everything he had, transforming their bedroom into a mini hospital, determined to save her.

I never thought I would pity him, but I did. After some time, I had to leave for better opportunities. On my last day, I glimpsed Stella—she lay motionless on the bed, the oxygen mask over face, her once vibrant spirit now muted.

Tears slid down my cheek as I walked away, leaving her, that house and town behind."

That old lady's strength seemed to drain away as she fell quiet, gazing out at the rain through the window behind me, lost in thought. Slowly, she took a sip of water and noticed the first candle had nearly burned out. She lit a second one. With a deep breath, she began to speak again.

"When I returned for Christmas break, after a few months, I noticed people whispering stories and blaming Stella and Mr. Hawkins for her condition. Everyone said they should have never given shelter to that child, claiming he had jinxed their happiness and her health. In a way, I found myself agreeing with them. Then the news broke, sending shockwaves through the entire town."
She fell still once more, this time for much longer.

'What news?' I wondered, the question burning in my mind, yet I didn't dare to voice it. The sorrow etched on her face was evident, and she seemed lost in a world of her own. I didn't want to disturb her reveries.

"You know what, Mr. White," her voice barely above a whisper, in a mournful tone. "Sometimes, I wish I had never worked there, never grown so close to her and the children. I wish I hadn't witnessed lengths a man would go, for the woman he loves, how far he would go to protect her. My life could have been different. I could have left this place long ago, but their memories—they hold me captive, refusing to let me go."

She rose slowly, moved to her right, and reached for the shelf. Her hands dug through a pile of dusty books until she unearthed a single, weathered piece of paper. She returned to her seat and handed it to me. It was an old newspaper clipping, the paper brittle and strained with age, its once white surface now faded to a brownish hue. In the dim candlelight, I leaned in, straining my eyes to decipher the words on that fragile paper.

I commenced to read aloud, my voice stable at first, but with each passing line, it began to waver. Soon, my words faltered and only my eyes continued across the page, tracing the sentences in silence. The words stuck in my throat, impossible to speak.

The Hawkins family is no longer alive

They were brutally murdered in their own house last night. Mrs. Stella Hawkins was discovered in the study room. She was choked and stabbed repeatedly until her life slipped away. The same happened with Mr. William Hawkins and their bodies were set on fire. Their 3-year-old son, Arthur, had been dismembered beyond recognition. The sole survivor was 17-year-old Gerald Walsh, the foster child who lay unconscious at The Beardwood Hospital.

Inspector Charles Ashford apprehended the prime suspect - the family's trusted doctor and close friend, Dr George Hart - just hours after the murders. The police are still grappling with the enigma of the motive behind this gruesome homicide, investigating into shadows and secrets that might unravel the twisted reasoning behind such a brutal act. They are also searching for the servant of the house, who has vanished without a trace, his disappearance adding another layer of mystery to the chilling crime. Was he part of it, too? Did he aid the doctor in this madness? Or he's also dead and not found? The police will find their answers only when they finally catch him or discover his body.

With Christmas just around the corner, this heinous act has cast a dark gloom over the town, shattering the festive spirit and leaving everyone in a state of shock.

The rain had ceased, leaving the scent of damp earth hanging in the air. I read the article again. I finally spoke with a startle.

"Gerald? He is still in that hospital. I have seen him." My words came out in a rush, disbelief strangling my voice. "Who is he? What's his story?" my hands shook, barely able to hold the weightless, crumbling a piece of newspaper. Despite the biting chill, sweat trickled down my forehead.

"Calm down," the old woman replied, her tone steady amidst the storm brewing in my mind.

"Water... please." My throat tightened. My house—its walls held horrors far worse than I ever imagined. Though I had known of the killings, the grim details left me reeling.

She poured a glass of water from the jar on the table in front of us, her movements deliberate before placing it in my unstable hand. "Yes," she continued, "Gerald—a sweet child with a heavy past, who lived in his own little world and barely talked to others, is still in a mental care facility. It's been years. He never recovered. It was not the first time that someone died in front of him.

The second abandoned house next to mine, once, he used to live there with his family—his mother, Bethany Walsh, and uncle Darron.

After her divorce, she moved here to live with her brother. Everything seemed fine at first—quiet, regular. Then one morning in 1968, my father noticed a foul stench creeping from their place, and that's when things began to unfold.

At first, he knocked, timid, hoping for some response—but silence was all he got. Days dragged on, the odour growing thicker, more suffocating, until we could bear it no longer. We informed Mr Hawkins about this and he called for help, and that was when I first saw Inspector Charles Ashford.

When we finally forced our way into the house, what we discovered froze us in our tracks. Gerald sat motionless on his knees in front of a candle, drenched in blood, reading a book. Beside him lay his mother, her lifeless body horrifically disfigured—divided in half."

"Did Gerald kill his mother?" I asked, losing my calm.

"He was only nine years old, Mr. White. During the investigation, the police discovered the true killer—Bethany's brother, Darron. He had fled the scene and vanished without a trace, eluding capture to this day. But the most startling part was when the autopsy unearthed something far more disturbing: Bethany had been killed twelve days before her body was found, but the mutilation of her body happened long after she was already gone.

However, no one had entered that house. Only Gerald was there. There's still uncertainty about how it all happened. I have the police report, though I'm not quite sure where I've put it. Give me a few days, and you can stop by—I'll make sure to have it ready for you.

Returning to the case, when the inspector gently asked how he had survived those days without food, Gerald's innocent reply made hearts skip a beat: *"Mother was feeding me."*

Was he eating her?

This question stayed like a curse. The police suspected it, but Gerald was too young to interrogate properly, leaving the horrors of those days unanswered. The town turned on him, branding him with cruel names—flesh eater, abyss-born, abomination. They demanded him to be cast out, but then Stella stepped forward.

With unwavering determination, she accepted Gerald, offering him shelter when no one else would. Whether she was brave or simply blind to the rumours, no one could say. But one thing was evident—her act of kindness restrained her from the deep secrets Gerald carried with him."

The room fell into a stifling pause.

"Why did Dr. Hart do what he did? What was the motive behind the killings? Did they ever find the servant? Was he part of it?"

"Dr. Hart confessed, saying on that particular night,

he was in the house and responsible for their deaths. It was his twisted revenge for being humiliated. I testified against him. The evidence was also damning enough to send him to life imprisonment.

As for the servant, he is still not found, and his involvement is still a puzzle. The entire police force was after him. They came close to catching him more times than they could count, but each time, he slipped through their grasp. Rumours swirled at the time—maybe he wasn't running from the police at all, but from the killer."

"This happened on December 23rd 1976?" I asked, noting the date on the newspaper was blurry.

"Yes," she replied and just then the clock in my house chimed its nightly toll, like always signalling midnight. It was clearly heard from this distance.

23 December, 1996
12:00 A.M.

She added, "Exactly twenty years ago."

CHAPTER FIVE

Things got Personal

12:30 A.M.

I returned to the Hawkins house to find the gate half open. Inside, Leslie sat on the couch, her face buried in her hands. My footsteps startled her, and in an instant, she was on her feet, rushing toward me. "Where were you? I was so worried!" she exclaimed, wrapping her arms around me.

Should I tell her the truth about this house? Its dark history loomed over us. "I went to the neighbour's." I concealed the truth again. "With Christmas coming up, I thought I'd invite her over."

"Fine, but is this really the right time to invite someone?" she muttered, glancing at the clock. "You could have done that tomorrow. Anyway, forget it. Let's eat—I'm starving!"

She seemed a little more at ease and walked toward the kitchen, just as Oliver appeared in the doorway, his face tense with worry. "You're back, Mr. White! I was looking for you everywhere."

"Yes, sorry for the trouble." I replied in a subdued tone. He acknowledged with a faint, understanding smile.

"Daddy, I was waiting for you! Look, I have done all the decorations. Are you happy now?" Liam called from behind, his voice a mix of excitement and exhaustion as he descended the stairs, his eyes half-lidded with sleep.

I smiled warmly and kissed his forehead. "I am so proud of you, son. You did a great job." Then, a sudden chill ran through me as I scanned the hall. My voice trembled as I asked-

"Where is your sister?"

"She wasn't in the room," Liam replied, his innocent eyes blinking up at me. My gaze shot to the study on the first floor, dread clawing at my gut. Without a word, I sprinted towards it.

The door was locked from the inside. I knocked, my breath hitching. "Ebba?" Silence. I pounded harder, my palm slamming against the wood. "Ebba, please open the door!"

Mrs. Stella Hawkins was discovered in the study room—strangled, jabbed and lifeless in flames.

The news replayed relentlessly in my mind as I banged on the door, each knock echoing my mounting desperation. Fear gripped me, an overwhelming terror that seemed to consume every inch of my being.

The door swung open, revealing Ebba standing there, her face had a mask of emptiness.

Leslie's voice peeled from downstairs. "Don't you know how to knock?"

I ignored her. My eyes were locked on Ebba, who returned my stare with a smouldering intensity, as if boiling with unspoken anger.

Leslie's voice pierced through again. "Come, dinner is ready!" which I neglected once more.

"Step out, Ebba. I need to lock this room," I said, trying to keep my voice steady.

"Why?" she asked, her expression flat and her tone was heavy.

"This room needs renovation. It is not safe here." I replied with calm.

"You are lying," she shot back, her eyes never wavering from mine.

"Come out," I ordered, my patience wearing thin.

She pivoted, peered into the room as if someone within had captured her attention. Then slipped back out without a word.

I closed the door with a decisive click of the lock, slipping the keys into my pocket with a sense of finality. As I turned, Ebba remained by my side, her gaze fixed on me with a blank, fearless stare.

1:45 A.M.

"That old lady is a bit creepy. She doesn't talk much, and I have caught her watching our house intently more than once." Oliver muttered as we sat in the dimly lit, quiet hall, with the woods burning in the fireplace. While everyone else had retreated to their rooms.

"I was with her for hours, yet I still don't know her name," I admitted.

"She didn't tell you?" His eyes widened with surprise.

"No, I forgot to ask," I said, and we both let out a nervous chuckle.

"Her name is Dorothy Miles," He replied.

"How do you know?" I questioned, a frown forming on my brow.

"It's written on a marble plaque beside her gate. You didn't see it?"
"I didn't!" I murmured, more to myself than to him, wondering how I had missed something so obvious.

"Can I tell you something, Oliver?" I asked cautiously.

He looked at me attentively, his eyes narrowing slightly. "What is it?" He paused before adding, "You can tell me anything."

"The thing I am going to tell you, it has to stay between us," I said in a hushed tone and glanced around the house, my eyes darting every corner, making certain we were truly alone.

"Yes, of course, sir. You have my word." His tone was serious.

"Make one more drink for me, then." I need to share what I had learned today; the burden of it was crushing and I couldn't bear to keep it to myself any longer.

I lit a cigarette, a rare indulgence, and also cradled a half-empty glass of whisky in my other hand. Slumping into the couch, I exhaled a cloud of smoke; the strain gnawing at me.

Oliver sat across from me, his eyes locked on mine, absorbing every word by the time the cigarette burned down to its filter. I had spilled the entire past of the house and he remained unwavering, listening with grim patience.

"I heard about the killings, but I never realised they were this monstrous." Oliver finally reacted in an alarmed tone.

"Same here," I replied nonchalantly, rising from the couch. Oliver followed suit. "Keep this with you. Give it to no one else but me." I handed him the study room key, my eyes sealing onto his.

Taking the keys, he said, "I'll dig deeper and find out more."

I nodded, and he turned to leave. As I ascended the stairs, I paused. Ebba stood at the top, shrouded in dark, her gaze fixed on Oliver like a predator on its prey.

"Ebba? Do you need something?" I asked cautiously.

She slowly turned her head towards me, a sinister smile spreading across her face before she headed towards her room without a word.

8:00 A.M.

The dark history of this house kept replaying in my mind like a broken record. I needed to push it aside, to drown it in something positive. But how?

"Mr. George Hart is innocent. He didn't kill the Hawkins family." Leslie's voice cut through the storm in my head as she walked into the room.

"What?" I shot up from the bed, my heart pounding. How did she know? Did Oliver tell her? I cussed myself for confiding in him, cussed the whiskey that loosened my tongue.

"Yes, it's on the front page of today's paper," she said, her eyes narrowing as she studied my reaction. "It's all over the news, but I have no idea what it means. Do you?"

Fought the urge to snatch the paper from her hands before she could read any further and forced a smile. "I might have heard about it somewhere, but I don't know the details."

Now wasn't the time to tell her—the truth would only make things worse.

She handed me the newspaper, her gaze drifting on me, searching for cracks in my facade.

"Do you know where Oliver is?" she asked unexpectedly.

"No, I don't," I replied

"God, he gave breakfast to kids and hasn't had his own yet. Such a careless boy. He could have at least woken me up." She muttered with a tinge of maternal frustration and walked out of the room, leaving me alone with the newspaper in my faltering hand.

I let out a shallow breath of relief, but only for a moment. I sat down to uncover what all the fuss was about. Everything was turned on its head.

4:30 P.M.

Leslie and I were seated at the dining table, listening to a few romantic songs on the radio, which is around 8 years old and still working fine, while Liam played with his toys in the garden and Ebba napped on the couch. Leslie's gaze shifted repeatedly between the main gate and the clock.

"Are you expecting someone?" I asked, noticing her restless glances.

"Oliver is still not home, and I am starting to panic. Did you give him any task or send him to the post office again?" Leslie asked, her voice fluttering with doubt.

"I haven't," I replied, doing my best to comfort her. "It's the festival season—he might have gone to visit relatives or friends. He will be back soon. Try to relax."

She switched off the radio and looked at me, silently pleading for reassurance.

"He is fine and safe, my love. Don't worry."

Suddenly, a soft, weird giggle broke the conversation. I turned to see Ebba, who had been napping, now wide awake and struggling to stifle her mysterious laugh. She fixed me with a confusing, almost unreadable look. Then she closed them again.

'Where are you, Oliver?' I wondered.

8:00 P.M.

The night had grown bitterly cold, the air thick with fog that wrapped the garden in a heavy cloak. It was getting late, too late, and Oliver still wasn't home. The chill gnawed at my bones as I paced restlessly, my eyes fixed on the empty road.

Leslie was in the kitchen, pretending to be busy with Christmas preparations. The kids had retreated to their rooms, unaware of the stress mounting outside. My patience was fraying fast.
Through the smothering haze of fog, I saw—a faint outline at first, a thin figure moving towards me. The smog made it hard to see the face, but I knew who he was.

I opened the iron gate with a creak that echoed in the quiet night, striding out to block his path. Relief showered over me, but it was quickly replaced by a rush of anger. My blood ran hot, my face flushing in contrast to the icy air.

He stopped in front of me, his gaze meeting mine, sensing my mood. He knew exactly why I was upset.

"You think this is a guesthouse?" I spat, fighting to keep my tone stable. "That you can come and go as you please, without informing anyone?"

"Sorry, Mr. White," Oliver muttered, his head hung low. "I should have told you."

"Where the hell were you? What was so important?"

He looked up at me, his eyes misty with something I couldn't quite read. "Did you see today's paper?"

"Yes, I did. What about it?"

"Dr. George Hart is innocent. That was the headline," he said quietly.

I stared at him, confused and growing testy. "So what? After these many years, does it really matter whether he is innocent or not?"

"It matters to Dr. Hart, now in the twilight of his life, still clinging to a fragile hope that justice will find him before it's too late." Oliver said, his voice tightening with seriousness. "It matters to everyone who lived through that time, who still remembers what happened here that night. People don't talk about it, but they haven't forgotten. And, sorry to say this, Mr White, but people like you—people who've come here and settled down will read this today, will forget about it tomorrow. Then, in ten years, when the 30th anniversary of those killings comes around, you will remember again. It's not your fault, but you fail to grasp just how severe this case really is.

The locals need answers. What if Dr. Hart is really

innocent? Suppose if the actual killer is still out there? What if the Hawkins family still hasn't got justice?"

There was something in his voice. His eyes bore into mine, demanding answers I didn't have.

"Dr. George Hart confessed to the killings," I said slowly, trying to break through to him. "He is not innocent."

He shook his head, frustration creeping. "The lead investigator, Charles Ashford, told the press, he believes Dr. Hart was framed."

I was stunned. "How do you know that?"

"Because I met him today," Oliver replied in an indifferent tone. "He didn't want his name to be printed."

I stepped back, trying to wrap my mind around what he was saying. "You met him? Where? How?"

He sighed, glancing away for a moment before meeting my gaze again. "Last night after you told me everything and went to bed, I couldn't stop thinking about it. The news this morning pushed me to do something. I then called the directory enquiry services from where I got his contact details. I found his address and went to meet him."

The night closed tighter around us, the force of

his words bearing down on me. Something dark, something old, was stirring. And whatever it was, Oliver had just dragged it back into our lives.

Leslie came rushing out towards Oliver, her voice quivering with joy.

"Thank god you are back, son. Where have you been?" Without giving him a chance to respond, she asked again, "Did you eat anything? You were gone all day."

She looked at him with a motherly concern that bordered on possessiveness, as if she wanted to adopt him right then and there.

After a brief exchange, Leslie, now satisfied, went inside. I wasted no time, my voice low and urgent.

"So, what did you find out from Inspector Ashford? Why does he think Dr. Hart is innocent?"

Oliver cleared his throat and began, "Inspector Ashford is 55 now. His memory is fading, but he still vividly recalls that night—December 23rd 1976. It was quiet, everyone preparing for Christmas, until around 2 A.M. when a young girl stormed into the police station, shaking with fear, barely able to stand."

Oliver paused, his eyes distant as he relived the tale. "She was terrified," he continued, "pleading for them to come with her, sobbing and gasping for breath. Inspector Ashford approached her, gave her a chair, a glass of water, and asked her to explain what happened. That's when she dropped a bombshell—'*The Hawkins family is in danger. If we don't hurry, they will die.*' "

I couldn't hold back. "Who wanted to kill them?"

Oliver's gaze sharpened, and replied, "The inspector asked the same question. Who wants to kill them? And then, she said something that still bothers him to this day—'*Mrs. Hawkins wants to kill everyone.*'

"What?!" My heart pounded in disbelief. "If she wanted to kill, then who killed her?"

"Exactly. That's the mystery. She couldn't have done that. She was not strong enough to overpower her husband. And no mother, not even the cruelest, could be capable of such monstrous evil against her own flesh and blood. Even Inspector Ashford found no evidence linking her to the killings."

We stood there, silence creeping in, both of us rattling by the unsettling revelation. Then I broke it.

"Why is the inspector so sure that Dr. Hart is innocent?"

"Years ago, Inspector Ashford met Dr. Hart after release for good behaviour. Then he told him, 'if you hadn't killed them, you wouldn't have wasted 17 years of your life in prison' and Dr. Hart only said one thing in response before walking away."

"What was it?" I asked.

"Inspector Ashford was taken aback when he stated, 'I wish I had killed them.' Inspector firmly believes that a man who has already served his sentence has no reason to lie."

Oliver paused, his face grim. "Now, with new technology, Ashford wants to reopen the case. The 20th anniversary of the murders gave him a chance to speak up. That's why he spoke to the press as well. Hoping that, at least, the truth would surface and the real culprit would finally step out from the shadows and reveal itself to everyone.

I tried to process everything, my mind spinning with more questions. "Who was the girl who warned the inspector?"

Oliver's brows furrowed as he searched his memory. "The cook. What was her name... Grace? Yes, Grace Radley."

"What?" I got fixed, my stomach knotting as I struggled to process it. "I think I know her... I've met her before."

Oliver's eyes widened. "Where?"

"There was a woman on the train with the same name. Acted strange when she found out we were going to live here, then vanished. It all makes sense now."

"Are you sure she's the same, Grace?"

"I am not, but there is a good chance. We can confirm it. She gave her address to Leslie."

"Perfect then. Tomorrow, we will go to meet her. If she's Grace from that night, she might have the keys to everything."

I nodded and asked, "So if it wasn't Dr. Hart, who does Inspector Ashford suspect?"

He leaned in, lowering his voice. "Even Ashford doesn't know for sure. Could be anyone, someone close, or maybe someone we haven't even considered yet. Someone completely off the radar."

I narrowed my eyes. "What do we know about the servant?"

"Carter," Oliver said, his tone darkening. "He worked here for over a decade. The night of the murders, he disappeared. No one's seen him since. He vanished without a trace. Nobody knows whether he's hiding or buried?"

Before I could react, a blood-curdling scream shattered the stillness of the night. It was Leslie.

We both bolted inside the house, hearts racing, terrified.

9:30 P.M.

We rushed inside the house, only to find Leslie stood in the middle of the hall, her eyes locked on the study room upstairs, wide with fear. Oliver and I followed her gaze, our steps slow and heavy, and what I saw was enough to make any parent's heart seize in sheer dread.

Ebba had Liam dangling over the railing, his feet suspended in mid-air, choking as her twisted smile spread across her face. Temper flashed in her hollow eyes. An unnatural sound escaped her throat, seeping into me with a paralysing intensity.

Leslie rushed for the stairs, and we followed, too stunned to comprehend what was happening.

Then, a voice-deep, distorted, not Ebba's screeched, "Don't come up, or who will save him when he falls?"

Leslie broke down, sobbing. "Ebba? Is this some kind of sick joke?"

But I knew it wasn't. I had seen the changes in her, felt the shift. Despite that, I did nothing.

Ebba's smile dissolved into fury as she glared at me. "How dare you? You said I couldn't go into my own room. You don't want to live?"

Halted with fright, I stammered, "What do you want, Ebba?"

"Ebba?" She let out a bone-chilling laugh and said, "I want the keys, Mr White."

I exchanged a quick look with Oliver, and he understood immediately. He rushed to his room, returned with the keys and passed them to me.

"Take them," I said, my voice trembling. But let my son go."

She glared at me, silent. I moved to the first floor and slid the keys towards her, praying it would end here. She picked them up, and in one motion, stretched her arm out—sending Liam over the railing.

Leslie screamed, and Oliver lunged, but it was too late. Liam fell.

Oliver scrambled to catch him, but Liam hit the ground hard. Blood pooled from his head as Oliver desperately tried to stop it. Leslie collapsed and was unmoving. I remained there, numb, watching as Ebba calmly unlocked the door, stepped inside the room, and sealed it from within.

In a matter of minutes, everything had slipped out of control, and now things got personal.

CHAPTER SIX

Round Table

24th December 1996
2:00 A.M.

The Beardwood Hospital

As I sat in the emergency room, watching Liam lie unconscious, surrounded by machines, the cold, rhythmic beeping seemed to mock the turmoil within me. Doctors hovered, their faces masked by concentration. I stood apart, helpless, a silent observer of my son's suffering.

Outside, Leslie sat on a bench, wiping away endless tears. Her face was pale, struggling to process the horror that had just unfolded. Her hands trembled as they rested in her lap and her eyes were lost in the void.

Dr. Alice's voice sliced through the tension, momentarily drowning out the steady beep of machines. "Mr White, you need to step out," she commanded, her tone firm.

My throat tightened. "Is he... is he going to be okay?" I struggled to keep the fear from breaking me.

"He will be fine. Trust me." She gestured toward the door, and I knew there was nothing more I could do. "Thank you for coming." I murmured, though the words felt hollow.

She acknowledged, turning her attention back to Liam as a nurse guided me outside. The door closed, sealing the gravity of the moment inside. I sank down beside Leslie. She glanced at me, her voice barely a mumble between sobs, "How's he?"

I couldn't speak. The silence between us was thick with dread. Her voice cracked as she whispered again, "Why did Ebba do this?" She buried her face in her hands, her shoulders shaking as she fought back sobs. "We never should have come here. This is all my fault."

Her words cut deep. I couldn't keep the secret any longer. Not now. "Leslie, it's not your fault. But there's something you need to know... something I should have told you long ago."

She looked at me with her tear-filled eyes, as I revealed all which was suppressed till now. For a while, everything got paused. The burden of it got lifted, but now it will drown us both. She shot to her feet, her expression hardening into something cold, something I hadn't seen before. She didn't speak at first, the silence was louder than the accusation.

"I know what I did was," I began, but before I could explain, she cut me off, her voice like ice.

"Leave."

"Leslie, please," I begged, but the storm in her eyes was unyielding.

"Leave!" she shouted, her voice echoing down the sterile corridor. I could feel the eyes of strangers on us, but they were nothing compared to her gaze, burning with betrayal.

Head Hanging, I walked away, knowing that I deserve it and now, I must find a way to make things right, no matter what.

The night thickened with smoke, each breath turning to mist in the frigid air. Leaving Leslie behind in the hospital, confident in her that she will manage, I returned home, where Oliver was watching over Ebba, still locked away in that room.

We settled in the hall, the stress palpable as we mapped out our strategy. For nearly an hour, we plotted and muttered, every word heavy with consequence, until we each knew our roles in the unfolding drama.

I hurried to my room, where I spotted Leslie's bag tossed on the floor. Dumping its contents onto the bed, I shifted through the clutter, searching for the slip of paper Grace had given her. My pulse raced as

I finally found it. Quickly, I stuffed everything back into the bag, added some extra cash and handed it to oliver.

"Take this to the hospital and give it to Leslie. You know what to do next," I said.

"Yes." he responded, grabbing the purse and disappearing out of the room without hesitation.

I unfolded the paper once more, my eyes scanning the address one last time: "37 Old Road, Ribble Valley"

If I left now, it would take me an hour to reach. But what about Ebba? What was I supposed to do with her? She needed me, but If I truly wanted to save her, I had to make tough choices. The reality of this mansion was still covered, and whatever happened with Ebba wasn't normal—she wasn't my daughter anymore. If I wanted her back, I needed to find a way.

I went to the study room, standing outside the door she had locked from the inside. With a heavy head, I secured an additional lock on the outside, ensuring Ebba would not leave while I was gone.

Left the house and sprinted straight to Dorothy's place, my eyes landing on the sign I hadn't noticed before—Dorothy Miles. I banged on the door, panic surging through me. "Dorothy, it's Aston!"

She opened the door, her drowsy eyes squinting at me. "Here it is," she said sharply, holding out a folded paper, irritation clear in her voice. "I told you to take it from me, but not now."

"What is this? What are you talking about?" I asked, confused, as I took the paper from her hand.

"The police report on Bethany's case," she replied, her tone biting. "Isn't this what you've pestered me for?"

"No."

"Then, what's wrong? Is everything all right?" Her frail sight may have failed her, but she could see the urgency and desperation written across my face.

I didn't waste time spilling the entire story and begging her to come with me.

"Oh God, I feared this would happen," she muttered, her drowsiness evaporating in an instant. With exigency in her steps, she went back inside to gather what she needed and I tucked the police report into my jacket pocket; there was no time to dwell on it now. Five minutes later, she emerged, wearing a proper gown, this time under a jacket. We left in a hurry.

The road stretched out before us, uncannily empty, flanked by dense, dark forest on both sides. Stiff wind bit at our faces, and the streetlights, shrouded in thick fog, cast weak halos of light, barely illuminating the path ahead. The beam from my torch was useless, swallowed by the mist. Despite it all, we pressed on, our footsteps fast.

"What are you planning to do?" Dorothy asked, her voice cutting through the muteness.

I was just about to answer when I heard it—a footstep, heavy and deliberate.

This one was different. Someone was walking behind us. I twirled around, eyes narrowing through the fog, and saw a shadowy figure trailing us. A cold knot twisted in my gut. Ignoring it, and quickening my pace. "You'll find out soon enough," I muttered, trying to mask my growing unease.

But then I realised something was unsettling—the figure trailing us was matching our pace. My instincts flared, and I stopped dead in my tracks. As expected, the figure halted too.

"What's wrong?" Dorothy asked, sensing the jitters.

"Wait." I turned back, eyes locked on the vague outline in the distance. I took a step towards the shadow, but before I could get close, the figure turned suddenly and slipped into the woods, vanishing into the trees. My heart pounded as I started into the gloom.

"Someone had been following us." I muttered under

my breath, wishing I had caught a glimpse of that face. Shaking off the moment, I came back to Dorothy, took her hand and continued walking until we arrived at 37 Old Road.

6:30 A. M.

The house loomed larger than I had expected, especially for a single woman. The area was posh too—far from what I imagine Grace could afford. Christmas decorations adorned the exterior in lavish detail, glowing softly in the mist. A stark contrast to the disrupting journey we had just made. Whoever lived here wasn't short of money.

"This is Grace's house," Dorothy said. She looked stunned. Unknowingly confirming my suspicion. She asked "You know her?"

"I am here to get to know her," I replied, catching my breath as we approached the door. I knocked, waiting in silence; nothing. I tapped again, more insistent this time, the seconds dragging on like hours. Finally, a voice answered from behind us, startling me.

"Yes, how can I help?" Grace stood there, her face was shadowed by fatigue, as if she had been running, too.

"Grace, it's me—Dorothy,"

"Oh, hey! It's been so long. How are you?" she said,

a hint of surprise and warmth in her voice.

"I am good! What about you?"

A soft smile touched her lips. "God has been kind. By the way, why are you here at this hour? Is everything all right?" she asked, her voice flat but curious.

"Actually, no, meet Mr Aston White," Dorothy said, motioning towards me. "He is the new owner of Hawkins' house."

Grace's eyes flicked with recognition, but not surprised. "The new owner", she said, almost to herself.

"She knows," I said, locking eyes with her. "You look exhausted."

Grace didn't flinch. She answered casually, "I go for a walk every morning at dawn," then she turned to face Dorothy and added softly, "It helps me keep my diabetes in check."

"Is that so?" I didn't press further, though I felt there could be more to it. I hadn't come here to chase her lies. My mind was already on what needed to be done next, hoping Oliver was staying on track while I dealt with what was in front of me.

Grace's tired gaze lingered on me, but there was something beneath it. "Are you not going to invite us in?" I asked politely, my voice steady, but mind racing.

Grace blinked, startled out of her thoughts. "Oh, of course. Please, come in," she said hurriedly, fumbling with the lock before guiding us inside.

As we stepped through the door, I was taken aback by the grandness of it all. The guest room was nothing short of extravagant. An oversized chandelier hung from the ceiling like a glittering sentinel, its light dropping softly on the room. The floor was covered in a plush, intricately designed Asian carpet. Furniture was crafted from imported wood, polished to a high shine. The walls, painted a crisp white, were adorned with hand made paintings that reeked of exclusivity and between them hung a certificate of appraisal from Manchester Crown Court, displayed proudly.

Everything about the place screamed—wealth; wealth that didn't add up for someone like Grace. How on earth could she afford this?

"Please, make yourselves comfortable. I will be back in a moment," Grace said with a forced smile. She disappeared down the hallway, leaving us alone in this grandeur.

Dorothy and I sat quietly, settling into the luxurious chairs. Four more chairs sat empty, as if waiting for an unseen audience. Minutes passed before Grace returned, balancing a tray with two glasses of water.

"You both must be parched after such a long journey," she said, offering the drinks. We accepted them without hesitation, gulping the water down, grateful for the brief relief.

"Would you like it more?" Grace asked, noticing how quickly we finished.

"No, no, we are fine," Dorothy answered, her voice wavering slightly. She glanced around, clearly nervous. "After all these years, we finally meet again. So, tell me, how's life treating you?" she asked gently with a smile.

I muttered under my breath, 'Just look around. What do you think? How's life treating her?' Silly question to ask.

Grace returned the smile. "I have something to tell you, by god's grace, I'm now a legal clerk at the Manchester Crown Court. So, all is as it should be. And you?"

"Likewise, and I'm truly happy for you." Dorothy responded. The lavish surroundings, and now this news. There was jealousy beneath the surface, but she concealed it flawlessly.

A pang of sympathy washed over me for Dorothy—her fragile, two-room house on the verge of collapse, with emptiness creeping in from each corner, her clothes tattered. Meanwhile, Grace stood in opposition, wrapped in the light of financial stability and comfort. They began their journeys side by side twenty years ago—one as a cook, the other as a babysitter. But now, it's painfully clear whose life has turned as the loser in the tale.

"I always knew, Mr White, you'd show up at my doorstep one day, but I never thought it would be this soon." Grace's voice shatters the delicate bubble of my thoughts, pulling me abruptly back to reality.

"You have no idea what happened," Dorothy started speaking on my behalf, her voice tight with urgency. She recounted the events that unfolded just hours ago at my house- the attack, the terror, the chaos that turned our lives upside down.

Grace's expression shifted, first to concern, then to something darker. Pity.

"Jesus! I am sorry to hear that," she said softly, sympathising with lacing her voice. "How is your son?"

"He is under the doctor's care. He will pull through," I replied, but lacked conviction.

"And your daughter?" she asked, but her tone carried a fearful edge.

I held up the words caught in my throat. What could I say? The silence stretched between us.

The line of questioning made me shift in my seat,

heat rising as I shrugged off my jacket. And that's when my eyes caught the page tucked into the pocket. I slid it out, my fingers hovering for a moment before unfolding it.

Suddenly, a screech pierced the quiet- the sound of a car skidding to a stop outside. The engine roared and then died. My heart jumped in my chest as the doorbell rang, the sharp sound echoing through the house.

Grace glanced at the clock - 7:22 A.M.

Her brow furrowed. "Who could that be at this hour?" she muttered to herself, rising from her seat.

As she moved towards the door, I tensed, unsure of what to expect. Dorothy and I leaned back, straining to catch a glimpse of the newcomers. When she opened it, I released a small sigh of relief. It was Oliver, but he wasn't alone.

Grace stood fixed at the threshold, her body stiff, her face draining of colour. Dorothy, who had been sitting calmly moments before, shot to her feet. It was as though time itself had stopped—Both of them remained there, eyes wide, unblinking, staring like they were looking at ghosts from the past.

The air thickened with an oppressive hush as two figures stood on the doorstep alongside Oliver. The weight of their presence was unmistakable. Their arrival carried a palpable dread seeping into every corner of the house.

Oliver gave me a subtle nod, signalling that his part was done, then quietly slipped away to head for the hospital. I hadn't anticipated him pulling this off so flawlessly, but he had and the reactions of both women were undeniable proof of it.

"Inspector Charles Ashford and Doctor George Hart," Grace whispered, her voice throbbing with disbelief.

"Let them in, Grace. They've come a long way," I said, breaking the tense stillness and cutting through the stiff stare.

By just one glance, it was clear who was who. Inspector Ashford, a slim man, wore an immaculately pressed blue chequered shirt over black trousers. Though well into his fifties, his sharp, sincere expression spoke volumes about the unwavering professionalism that still defines him.

Doctor Hart, on the other hand, stood just as tall, around six feet, but his bloated frame and sagging, tired face—marked by deep wrinkles and the dark shadows under his eyes—were reminders of the seventeen brutal years he had spent behind bars. As they settled in, I shook hands with each of them before returning to my seat. Meanwhile, Grace and Dorothy remained suspended. Their unease was clearly visible.

Grace was confused, while Dorothy's gaze was locked on Dr. Hart, her eyes burning with a mix of anger and disgust; she still believed he was the killer. From what I knew about her, she also must be revelling in a sense of pride, knowing all too well that her testimony had been the one to seal his fate, condemning him for nearly two decades in prison.

Sensing the pressure, I motioned for the two women to sit down, assuming the role of host. They obeyed and soon the five of us were seated in a tight circle, the glass coffee table standing as the only thing between us. Dorothy sat to my right, Grace on my left. Directly across from me, the doctor occupied the seat, Grace's left. While Inspector Ashford was positioned on Dorothy's right. An empty chair separated the two men. It's time for the roundtable discussion.

To end the suffocating silence, I cleared my throat and spoke, keeping my voice controlled. "Everyone, my name is Aston White. We have gathered here for one reason—to uncover the answers that have eluded us for too long. We all have our own truths to seek, but now it's become personal for me. My family is now involved, and I need to know what really happened."

"I don't want to dig any of this back up—let bygones be bygones," Grace said immediately, her voice strained as she shot to her feet.

"I don't believe in any of this, but I think my

daughter is possessed and there's a chance it all ties back to that night—**December 23rd, 1976.** I need to know how to help her. So please," I urged, my eyes locked on Grace.

Without hesitation, she replied, "Take her to a doctor or a priest, but don't drag me into this. I can't help, Sorry." She turned away, her cold indifference a sharp contrast to the sweet woman I'd met on the train.

Just as frustration threatened to boil over, Inspector Ashford cut in with a calm but commanding voice. "Tell me how I can help."

A flicker of hope reignited within me.

"Why are you all so bothered?" Grace said, her voice pointed. "Trust me, we all are just wasting our time..."

She kept talking, but I wasn't listening anymore. My fingers tightened around the paper I had been holding for too long. Slowly, I unfolded it.

Crime Report

Bethany's Case

1. Police Department: Whalley Police Service
2. Case Number: 001258
3. Date and Time of Report: 3rd January 1969, 14:30
4. Location of Incident: Woodland Street, Whalley
5. Reporting Officer: *Inspector Charles Ashford*
6.Crime Category: *First-Degree Murder*
7.Witness: *William & Stella Hawkins*
8.Date & Time of Crime: *23rd December 1968, Between 01:00 AM-05:00 AM*

Details of Incident:

The call came through on 999—Emergency number. William Hawkins, in an edgy voice, reported a foul stench seeping from the house next door. It had been growing stronger for days. The door was locked from the outside, but something about it felt wrong—he feared the worst.

Inspector Charles Ashford arrived soon after with his team to find a restless crowd gathered outside the house, cooking their own stories. When the door was broken open, they found dead Bethany Walsh lying on the floor, her body cruelly sliced in half and covered with vicious knife wounds, signs of torment before death. The only survivor was her 9-year-old son, Gerald, sitting silently in the corner drenched in blood. But one person was missing—Bethany's brother, Darron Collins.

The neighbours—Mr & Mrs Hawkins, highly regarded figures of the town stepped forward as a 'Fact Witness'. The evidence was secured—blood stains, a weapon still smeared with red, and the chaos of a violent struggle. It all screamed of a calculated act fuelled by rage or pure insanity.

Findings:

For now, Darron Collins is the prime suspect. But another name had surfaced—Bethany's ex-husband, Rodrick Walsh. Their bitter divorce had left him with a hefty alimony to pay, and Gerald had gone to live with her. The investigators couldn't ignore the possibility as they dug deeper. His recent behaviour and connections came under the microscope.

Was this his way of escaping the financial burden and getting his son back? Or was there something darker driving him? The truth is still hidden, but the hunt is on.

Was this a crime committed by one person, or were there others involved in this chilling act? What was the actual motive? We got the puzzle pieces; soon, they will fall into place.

Action Taken:

Crime scene was examined and sealed; fingerprints and other forensics requested.

Status:

Under Investigation: The case remains clouded in mystery, with more questions than answers. But one thing is certain—justice won't rest until the truth is brought to light, no matter how dark or twisted it may be.

—

How is this even possible?

Both witnesses are dead.
Both crimes happened on *December 23rd*.
The same investigator is on the case.
The prime suspects in each case are still nowhere to be found.

Coincidence? A plan crafted with precision? Or could this be part of a larger conspiracy?

The pieces don't add up. Too many questions and the answers are hidden somewhere with someone—deep and dangerous.

I tucked the paper back, my mind racing. Then, a firm voice cut through the silence. "What do you want to know, Mr. White?"

Questions clawed at me, but I let the moment hang. Then, I met his eyes. "Everything, Inspector Charles." My voice was steady. Unwavering.

CHAPTER SEVEN

Truth or Deception?

7:15 A.M.

For a brief moment, a hush hung in the room, heavy and unbroken. No one spoke a word. Then, once more, Grace began to grumble.

"If you really want to know, go read the case file at the station," Grace snapped, irritation lacing her tone. "What can we say that hasn't already been said?"

I met her distant gaze, unflinching. "I would've done that already if the truth was in that file." I pointed towards the inspector. "Two decades later, the lead investigator still believes Dr. Hart wasn't the killer."

Dr. Hart's soft, steady voice broke through for the first time, his eyes downcast. "I think Grace is right. This doesn't make any sense."

"Exactly my point," Grace chimed in, a smug smile creeping across her lips.

"Dr. Hart," I pressed, locking eyes with him. "Did you kill them?

All eyes turned to him, but he said nothing, his head dropping once again into the familiar shadow of guilt and pain.

"Say yes, and I'll end this—right here," I said, voice tight.

He remained silent. The tension grew thick, pressing down on us. I shifted my sight to Grace, but for once, she had no retort.

Inspector Charles finally spoke, remorse thick in his voice. "I know he didn't kill anyone. Twenty years ago, I made a mistake—one I'll regret for the rest of my life. I'm sorry, Doctor."

"But I saw him that night," Dorothy interrupted, her voice shaking. "He came out of the house in a panic—blood on his clothes, terror in his eyes. He slipped into his car and sped into the night, tires screeching as he vanished down the road. Just minutes before, the wail of sirens signalled the arrival of the police. Can he explain what he was doing there that night?"

Dr. Hart remained silent. No defense. No denial. Then, Inspector Charles stepped in firmly. I'm certain of one thing—he paid for a crime that was never his to begin with."

Dorothy's eyes flared with disbelief. "You are letting your emotions cloud your judgment, Mr Ashford. What about the evidence? You can't ignore that! He was caught trying to flee at the railway station, wasn't he? Waiting for the next train to escape. If he did nothing, then he should have come to you. He killed Stella!" Her voice cracked.

Dr. Hart's voice broke through the conversation, laced with pain and quiet fury. "I killed no one. I was in the wrong place at the wrong time." Tears welling in his eyes.

"You confessed." Dorothy spat, her voice was swaying with emotion.

"I had to," he uttered quietly, the raw edge of suffering cutting through his words. "The interrogation was brutal, the torture unbearable. I denied it for weeks, kept telling them that I didn't kill them, but no one listened. Eventually, I lost hope and strength to fight for myself." Tears slid down his cheeks.

The atmosphere became tranquil. Even Dorothy couldn't meet her eyes now, the heft of his words sinking into the room like a leaden cloud.

Inspector Charles moved to sit beside him, placing a hand on his shoulder. "I should have listened to you, doctor. I can't give you back the 16 years you lost, but I can try to give you your dignity. The people in this town need to know that you are not the killer."

He looked at Dorothy, making sure that she heard.

While the others were swept up in the emotion, I remained focused. I realised it wouldn't be simple to dig up the secrets, not after all these years. But I wasn't here for Dr Hart. I was here to find out what had happened so I could protect my family.

"Dr. Hart," I asked, my voice cutting through the tension. "Can you help me to understand why my daughter, Ebba, has started acting strange? She's withdrawn, stopped speaking to us, and now she spends all her time locked in the study. She's grown obsessed with that room."

Grace's face paled. "The room where Stella was found dead?"

"Yes," Dorothy confirmed, her voice barely above a whisper.

"Oh Lord," Grace muttered, shaking her head. "Stella Hawkins showed the same signs at first. She was a vibrant woman, but over time, she grew distant, stopped talking to anyone, even ignoring her own child. Arthur was barely a toddler, and she shut him out completely. Then she got worse—aggressive. One day, she even tried to throw Arthur from the first floor, but Mr Hawkins stopped her and kept him safe. That's when the doctors told him she was mentally unwell, dangerous even. He made the decision to admit her to a hospital after Christmas. But before he could..." Her voice trailed off, the rest left hanging in the air like the ghost of a memory.

"Mrs. Hawkins' madness seeped into her elder son, Gerald," Grace continued, her voice lowering as if the walls themselves might hear. "He started behaving just like her—withdrawn, secretive. They'd lock themselves in a room for hours, reciting something, though none of us ever knew what. The night of the murders, everything seemed normal. I was in the kitchen, Carter was in the hall busy with decoration, and Mr. Hawkins was in the hall. Stella was upstairs, locked in her room, supposedly asleep, and children were in their room.

It was exactly 10 at night. The temperature was dropping, leaving a numbing frost.

'Grace!' Mr. Hawkins called, his voice steady as he sipped his drink. 'Bring the fruits.'

It was a routine—every night; he sliced fruits for Stella. Her dinner was limited to that and a glass of milk. Doctors' orders. No heavy food, especially at night. I carried the fruit tray outside, placing it in front of him alongside a knife. He didn't look up, not until he spoke again, this time addressing Carter.

'Have you given her the medicine?' he asked. His tone was calm, yet filled with anticipation.

Carter hesitated, his eyes flickering for just a second before answering, 'No.'

The air shifted. Mr Hawkins removed his reading glasses, the weight of his frustration slowly rising. 'And why not?' His voice was tight now, struggling to keep control.

'It's over,' Carter replied after a pause. 'I forgot to bring more.'

A dark fury surged through Mr. Hawkins. He stood, his face flushed with rage. 'After Christmas, she's going to the hospital. Can we at least do our duties until then, without fail?' His voice thundered through the room, a simmering anger that made both Carter and I look down, unwilling to meet his glare.

Without another word, Mr. Hawkins stormed to the landline sitting on the glass table, fumbling with the phone index as he dialled. He pressed the receiver to his ear, but nothing came through. 'Why isn't it working, Carter?' His voice was bitter now.

'I don't know, Mr. Hawkins,' Carter answered quietly.

'Then what do you know?' Mr. Hawkins roared, slamming his hand on the table with such force that it shattered the glass and blood began to trickle from his wrist. He didn't seem to care. His anger outweighed any pain.

His eyes briefly met mine, cold and unfeeling. 'Grace, you cut the fruit and take it to Stella on time.

I hope you're not as careless as him,' he said, his breath heavy, trembling with the effort to contain his fury.

'I will,' I managed to say, my voice barely more than a buzz.

'Good. I'm going to get the medicine.' He turned to Carter, eyes hard. 'Bring me a scarf and a jacket from my wardrobe. And check the safe. Make sure it's locked.'

Without a word, Carter hurried upstairs. Mr Hawkins barely glanced at the deep gash on his wrist. 'You sit with Stella, Grace,' he instructed, already halfway out the door. 'Make sure she eats.'

'Yes, Mr. Hawkins.' I bent down, gathering the fruit that had fallen onto the floor, but my eyes couldn't help but linger on the blood pooling around his feet. 'You're bleeding,' I said, my voice weak. 'Let me get the first aid kit.'

'No need. It's nothing.' His voice was cold and dismissive. 'Do what's told. And tell Carter to bring the car keys.' I obeyed, leaving him behind as I followed Carter upstairs. When I entered Stella's room, she was lying still on the bed, her eyes closed, as though uninformed to the chaos downstairs. But something caught my attention. Carter was by the wardrobe, taking out the clothes, but then he turned toward the safe. He twisted the knob, and with a soft click, it opened. Inside, bundles of cash, gold bars, jewellery, and important papers gleamed in the low light. But instead of locking it as Mr. Hawkins had ordered, Carter left it open deliberately.

My heart raced. What was he doing? He slipped the car keys into his pocket, but as he pulled his hand out, something fell. A small bottle of pills. The same pills he'd been giving Stella every night. My blood ran cold."

"But he said it was finished," Dorothy asked, her voice breaking the silence. "Did he lie?"

"Yes," Grace replied, "He did."

"But why?" she probed.

"I have no idea," Grace answered, the words biting her tongue. "I still don't know why he did what he did."

Dorothy looked at me suspiciously, but before she could speak again, Doctor Hart intervened. "And then?" he asked softly, urging her to continue.

"Within minutes, Mr. Hawkins left the house, and Carter returned to his room. I cut the fruit and set the knife aside. Then called out to Stella to wake her. She was in a deep sleep, but as I gently shook her, her eyes snapped open—wide, unblinking, terrifying. I stepped back, scared. 'Come on, sit up,' I forced a smile, picking up a slice of apple. 'I'll feed you myself tonight.'

But something in her gaze was wrong, twisted. I told her I'd forgotten the milk and that I will be back in a minute. She said nothing, just kept staring at me, eyes hollow and distant.

Downstairs, as I was heading to the kitchen, Carter suddenly appeared, dressed as if he was ready to leave, a backpack and leather bag in hand. 'Where are you going?' I asked.

'To my house. Christmas is coming,' he said, his tone clipped cold. 'But you're supposed to leave in the morning,' I insisted, trying to understand.

'Don't tell me what to do, Grace,' he yelled.

Something was wrong. He wasn't himself. 'At least stay for dinner,' I pleaded. 'You know I've got no one else here.'

For a moment, he softened, turning back towards his room to drop his bags. I felt a brief relief—until the house filled with Arthur's cries, piercing and desperate.

'Carter!' I called out. 'I need your help—Arthur's up!'

He rushed over, irritated. 'I'm not good with kids. You go,' he said, pushing the bottle towards me.

'Take the bottle and make sure he sleeps,' I insisted. 'I need to feed Stella.'

Reluctantly, he agreed, but as I returned to Stella's room, dread settled in my stomach. She wasn't in her bed. I checked the bathroom—nothing.

'Carter!' I shouted, my voice cracking.

He appeared from the hallway, holding Arthur's milk bottle, panic rising in his eyes. 'The children's room is locked from the inside,' he said, his voice tight.

I ran back to Stella's room, my heart tearing. The knife I had set aside—it was gone.

'Carter,' I screamed, my voice trembling. 'Stella's not in her room. And the knife—it's missing.'

His eyes widened. 'What do you mean?'

'I forgot to lock the door,' I stammered, fear choking my words.

Me and Carter stood outside the children's room, fear tightening its grip on us, unsure of our next move. Arthur's cries ceased, the house fell mute. Just then, a soft sound of something rippling reached our ears—a faint, liquid trickle. We lowered our eyes to our feet, and there, seeping from under the door, was a slow, steady stream of blood. I felt numb until the clock chimed, its echoing bell cutting through the silence like a haunting warning we couldn't ignore, pulling me back to my senses.

Horrified, Carter and I exchanged a look—we

couldn't believe what we were seeing. He rammed his shoulder against the door, trying desperately to break it down, but it wouldn't budge.

'I'm calling the police!' I cried, turning to flee.

'Grace, no! Listen to me!' Carter shouted after me, which I had to ignore, and headed directly to the police for help."

Dr. Hart darted his eyes on me, as fearful stillness settled over the room. The gravity of Grace's words pressing down like a storm about to break. Inspector Charles finally broke the silence, his voice low but sharp. "And when exactly did you leave for the police headquarters?"

Grace hesitated, her eyes flickering with uncertainty. "It must've been around 1A.M.," she answered.

"As you mentioned, you heard the clock's bell," I began, with complete focus. "That clock chimes only at midnight. It means that when you heard the sound, it was 12 A.M. and immediately after, you left. So, you didn't leave at 1 A.M.—you left between 12 and 12:10, didn't you?"

Grace blinked, her composure slipping for just a second. "I'm not sure," she muttered, a slight tremor in her voice. "I wasn't in my senses... maybe I left around 12 A.M. So what?" Her tone grew defensive, almost desperate.

Inspector Charles exchanged a glance with me with a look that said something was off, something didn't add up. He straightened up in his seat. His gaze was intense. "What took you so long to reach us, Grace? The distance between the house and the police station is only 4.5 kilometres. Even if you were walking, it shouldn't have taken more than 45 to 60 minutes, yet you took nearly 2 hours."

Her eyes flickered, and she hesitated. "It was foggy," she said slowly, choosing her words with care. "Visibility was almost nothing. And on top of that, I have dyspnoea. I had to stop frequently to catch my breath."

Charles wasn't buying it. His fingers tapped impatiently on the table. "That doesn't explain why it required so much time."

Grace's lips pressed into a thin line, her defences visibly cracking, but she remained firm in her explanation.

Then Dorothy spoke up, her curiosity cutting through the strain. "Dr Hart, why did you go there that night?"

Doctor Hart took a deep breath, recalling the night in vivid detail. "I was sitting in my drawing room," he started untangling his version of the story, his voice quieter now, as if speaking would disturb the delicate balance of the room. "I was having coffee in my living room when I heard the doorbell. It was

11:10 P.M. When I opened it, there was William Hawkins, shivering in the cold, his hands shaking and looking desperate.

I was stunned—seeing him after all these years hit me like a shock, leaving me momentarily speechless.

I invited him in, and we took a seat. That's when he disclosed the reason for his visit. He needed medicines—urgently. For Stella. All the pharmacies were closed, so he came to me. I fetched the pills and handed them to him. But when we shook hands, something wasn't right.

I noticed blood; he was bleeding. There was a deep cut in his hand, right on his hypothenar eminence"

"Hypothenar... what?" Dorothy asked with curiosity.

"Here..." Dr. Hart pointed to the fleshy part of his palm beneath the little finger and continued.
I cleaned his wounds and bandaged him up. He was ready to leave now. For twenty minutes, he had stayed, but we had barely exchanged words. As I opened the door, he paused, his voice low yet heavy with emotion.

'I'm a coward, George,' he said. 'Never had the courage to apologise to you. I always push people away, especially those who pray for me and wish me well. I'm sorry, my friend. You know, there are so few I can truly call mine.' His words were raw and unfinished. There was more he wanted to say—I could see it in his eyes—but he held back. Behind his apology lay something deeper, a loneliness he couldn't bring himself to fully reveal.

'Whiskey?' I asked, unsure of what else to say. I knew him better than he knew himself—he never said no to whiskey. But he had changed; his priorities were now clear.

'I'd love to sit together like old times,' he said, his voice softer than usual. 'But I need to take these pills to Stella. Why don't you come with me?'

I shook my head. 'You go ahead. I'll join you in about an hour once I finish up here.'

He nodded, gave a faint smile, hugged me, and left. As the door closed behind him, his words stayed there with me.'

Dorothy kept her eyes fixed on the floor, the burden of guilt seeming to settle over her. I wanted to tell her that it wasn't entirely her fault—anyone else in her position would have done the same thing.

Dr. Hart resumed. "The clock struck 12:55 A.M. as the car rolled to a stop in front of the house; the engine was cut, and I stepped out. Everything had fallen into a hushed calm. Dalmore in hand, I moved toward the house.

I pushed open the iron gate, my steps quickening. The front door was ajar, swinging open with a low creak. A heavy thud echoed in my chest as I stepped inside, only to come to an abrupt halt. What I witnessed that day still haunts me to this very moment.

William lay on the floor of the hall, motionless, bleeding. My breath caught in my throat. Panic surged through me. I rushed to him, set the whiskey down on the floor. Reached out with unsteady hands and pressed my fingers to his wrist, searching for a pulse. He was still alive. Barely.

Where are the others? I pondered, felt my chest ache as I charged up the stairs, taking them two at a time. First, I checked the bedroom—empty. Then reached the children's room. Door was locked from inside, and my eyes fell on the blood pooled on the floor. A cold realisation clutched me: *William wasn't the only victim.*

I rammed the door with my shoulder, but no luck. Desperation clawed at me. "Gerald?" I called out, my voice fluttering. Silence answered me back.

Time was slipping through my fingers like sand. I dashed to the study room in panic. And there she was—Stella. My worst fear stood before me, real and undeniable. Just like William, she had been stabbed over and over. Blood soaked her lifeless body, her eyes staring blankly at the ceiling. There was nothing I could do to save her, watching as life fading from her. Soul drifting away.

The world tilted on its axis. Who could have done this? How had it all come to this? My mind was screaming for clarity but there was no time to dwell on questions. Needed to call for help—an ambulance, the police—before this agony completely consumed me.

The telephone. I turned and sprinted downstairs. Lifted the receiver and figured out—the phone wasn't working. I was just about to leave the house to get support when I heard footsteps on my left. Instinctively, I pivoted and saw him emerging from his room, carrying two heavy bags. Our eyes met—his detached, calculating.

'Carter!' I said, but the words hardly left my lips before something struck me from behind. Pain exploded in my skull, my vision blurring as I collapsed beside William, the world spinning into darkness. As I lay there, slipping in and out of consciousness, I saw Carter approach, his face expressionless. He's going to kill me, I thought, bracing for the end."

Dr. Hart's voice wavered, his eyes distant as he recounted the horrors of that night.

"I can't understand why he chose not to kill me. It would have been better if he had," he muttered. "Carter should have finished me off that fatal night"

I leaned forward, my voice low. "Who attacked you, Dr Hart? Who was it?"

His face twisted in frustration. "I don't know. I didn't see."

"Then why did they let you live?" I asked. "If Carter was the killer, why not silence you, too? You saw him. You could expose everything."

Hart's eyes met mine, haunted. "Maybe he was too confident, convinced that he could get away with it, even if he left me alive. Or he thought the police would never believe me. Maybe he assumed they'd blame me, take me for the suspect. Or his grudge was with the Hawkins family alone. But I'm convinced that the person who struck me from behind is also responsible for killing William and his family. It could go one of two ways: Carter was either helping that person, or he became the fourth victim." He halted, nervously tapping his foot.

"What happened next?" Dorothy asked.

Dr. Hart locked eyes with her, a brief but intense connection, before he began speaking. "I gasped, choking on the thick, suffocating smoke as I stumbled back to my senses. My eyes darted to William—the fire had claimed him. I ripped off my sweater, trying to smother the flames, but it was useless. Now it was too late. He was gone. I looked up, smoke billowing from the study room as well. I was aware of what happened, but had no strength or grit to go and witness her burning, too. It was too late. They were gone." Dr Hart's voice quivered, eyes hollow. "I stood there in the hall, petrified, in front of the haunting flicker of flames, with two burning bodies in that house. It was the same spot where William had humiliated me all those years ago, and now, in that moment, all the grudges, the rage, and the desire for revenge burned away with him. I picked up the bottle of Dalmore and set it beside his body. 'Look what I got for you—it's your favourite. I can't wait for us to meet soon and share it together. It'll feel just like old times.' Tears blurred my vision as I wiped them away, forcing myself to stay calm.

I lost track of time, but then my eyes landed on the clock—2:57 A.M.

I sprinted for the car, heart beating fiercely, and sped off into the night. I knew I should've gone to the police, but fear held me hostage. Instead, I made up my mind: I'd disappear for a few days and hide somewhere far from this place. Maybe then, everything would blow over... maybe. Little did I know I can't outrun my fate."

Doctor Hart concluded his account, but a nagging doubt crept in. Were the good doctor recounting the truth, or weaving a tale to suit his own end? With Carter gone, there was no one left to challenge his version of events.

"There's something I'd like to know," I said firmly, directing my full attention to Doctor Hart. "How did you all become friends? And what was the bond like between the three of you?" I asked, not out of curiosity, but to observe closely where he might slip up.

"Me and William were family friends." Doctor Hart started explaining, "His father, a stern army man, was often away, leaving him to spend most of his time at my house. Whereas Stella became part of our group during high school. I had seen them through it all—their brightest days and darkest hours.

At 19, they made their relationship official. By 1961, just two years later, they were married, and for a time, life seemed perfect. But it wasn't until 1973, when their son Arthur was born, that their family truly felt complete. That day was the peak of their happiness—a fleeting joy I didn't realise would vanish far too soon.

Is there anything else you'd like to ask, Mr. White? Please, if you still have doubts." He remarked in a sarcastic tone.

"Nothing for now," I replied, before turning to Inspector Charles. "Could we hear your side of the story, please?"

Inspector Charles made a slight coughing sound and began, his tone was grim. "It was around that time, just after the doctor had left, that I arrived at the house with Grace and my team. We discovered William's and Stella's bodies, brutally burned. Our primary concern was figuring out what had happened to the children. Then we forced open the children's room." He paused, swallowing hard. "Arthur was in his crib, his throat slashed, fingers severed, and his stomach riddled with stab wounds. In the corner, we found Gerald sitting, muttering something under his breath. We pulled him out and rushed him to the hospital. He's never been the same since. The others were sent to the morgue for autopsy.

In our investigation, we discovered that cash, gold, jewellery, and a number of critical documents were missing from the safe. Grace accused Carter, but we couldn't prove it," the inspector explained, his voice intense but distant.

"Why didn't you investigate the unknown person who attacked Doctor Hart?" I asked, my mind swarming with questions. And this was just the start.

He sighed. "At first, we didn't believe what the doctor was claiming. We assumed he made it up to cover his own tracks. But even after putting him through intense interrogation, his story never changed. We followed the leads... but it went nowhere."

I leaned forward, not satisfied. "And Carter? He wasn't a seasoned criminal. How did you lose him?"

"We did everything we could. He was sighted in multiple cities, but always managed to slip away before the local police could catch him. Eventually... the trail went cold."

I wasn't expecting such evasive answers from the man in charge of the investigation. The room was tense, all eyes focused on our exchange. My heart was hammering with the unspoken weight of what I knew.

"Where was he from?" I pressed.

"Birmingham," he answered curtly.

"Who was in his family?" I continued, determined.

"He had a sick wife and a son," the inspector replied, his tone growing uneasy.

"You didn't interrogate them?" I asked, the question laced with disbelief.

"We did. His wife swore she had no idea where he'd gone. We conducted months of surveillance on her, but it also didn't help. His son was a teenager, but she wouldn't let us speak to him. She didn't want the boy to know his father was a murderer."

I paused, feeling the pressure mounting. "Do you remember Carter's last name?"

He hesitated, searching his memory, but before he could respond, Grace spoke, her voice cutting through the silence like a knife. "White. His name was Carter White. Oh, lord" she realised.
The moment she said it, every head snapped toward

me, eyes wide with disbelief. The room felt stifling as the revelation I had concealed for so long hovered over us.

I exhaled slowly, steadying myself before breaking the silence. *"Carter White is my father."*

A stunned silence followed. They exchanged uneasy glances, but all their eyes came back to me, waiting for answers I wasn't sure I could give. I could feel their eyes on me, waiting for an explanation.

"When I was eight, my father first mentioned Hawkins' house to me, telling me about his work there. When he showed me a picture of it, I was completely captivated, mesmerised by its beauty and intricate details. At the time, I dreamed of owning it someday. But as I grew older, life happened, and that dream slowly faded into the background.

Years passed, and I settled into the monotony of a middle-class life, slowly suffocating in the boredom of it all. Then one day, Leslie—my wife, a government nurse—told me she was being transferred to Whalley. I didn't want her to go alone, so I started house hunting for our family.

The broker flooded my mailbox with photos and details of unique properties, each more forgettable than the last. But none of them called me until finally he sent the pictures of Hawkins' house. At that moment, the memories of my childhood came flooding back.

He told me about the murders, how no one wanted to touch the place, but for me, it was more than just a house—it was an unfinished piece of my past. I had to have it. It was as if fate had brought me full circle, returning to the place where my father worked all those years ago. I didn't plan this. It was all destiny that led me to this town, to that house... and to everything that followed."

All eyes were on me, filled with curiosity. The room remained silent until Inspector Charles broke it in an empathetic tone. "It's difficult to live without a father, especially when his whereabouts remain unknown."

The others all nodded in agreement.

"If you ever need my help, do let me know," Inspector Charles offered, his tone laced with a thin layer of pettiness.

I didn't hesitate. "I need your help right now, Inspector Charles," I replied firmly, but I made sure he heard the urgency beneath it.

His brow furrowed slightly, though he tried to mask his surprise. "Tell me," he replied, the casual disinterest faltering as he leaned in, waiting.

"The Bethany Murder Case." The words left my lips, and I felt the room shift—like the air had thickened, heavy with unease. No one had expected me to bring it up.

"What about it?" he asked, confusion flashing across his face.

"What if we're looking at this all wrong? Could the two cases be connected? Where's the missing link—the piece that ties it all together?" I uttered.

"For god's sake, let's put an end to this, Mr.White." Grace's crisp tone rang out. Her irritation was palpable as she stepped into the conversation.

I brushed her off and continued, "I need details from you about it."

"You already have Bethany's case report. I gave it to you, didn't I?" Dorothy said, glaring at me. I tilted my head ever so slightly—enough for her to understand without words. Stop. And she left it at that, saying nothing further.

Dr. Hart, silent until now, finally spoke. "If you've got the report, what more do you want?" His voice was edged with suspicion, his gaze darting between me and Dorothy.

The inspector studied me for a bit too long. Finally, with a slight shrug, he muttered, "Go on, I'll give you what you need." His tone was flat, his face unreadable.

"Rodrick Walsh," I said, leaning forward slightly.

"What do we know about him?"

Hearing the name, Grace visibly stiffened, her eyes fixed on Inspector Charles, holding something unspoken.

Inspector Charles exhaled deeply, running a hand down his face, the weight of old memories noticeable in the lines etched into his skin. "He wasn't involved," he said finally, his words careful and measured. "Let me make that clear. Rodrick Walsh was a barrister who has now assumed the role of president at Manchester Crown Court—a respected, powerful man. Untouchable. Bethany was his second wife, and at the time of the murder, he wasn't even in town. We explored every possibility, every lead. Nothing tied back to him. Nothing at all." He paused, his voice faltering slightly. "In the end, we had to close it."

My eyes instantly shifted to the wall in front of me.

MANCHESTER CROWN COURT

Certificate of Recognition

This certificate has been presented to **Grace Radley**
We appreciate your invaluable service and cooperation.
Presented by: **Rodrick Walsh***(President)*

—

Everyone turned to see where I was looking, and things got clear—she was connected to him.

"I think it's best if you all leave now. Please," Grace said, her voice impatient. She could sense what was coming her way.

"Alright," I said with a smile, rising from my seat, putting on the jacket.

I didn't find her behaviour strange. She was losing control of the situation and knew it. Now, questions would come her way—questions she might not be able to answer.

We all came out, and before leaving, Dorothy extended her arm toward Doctor Hart, her voice heavy with regret. "I misunderstood you. Because of me, you suffered a lot—for 16 years. My apology won't change anything; the damage has already been done."

Dr. Hart replied, "You did nothing wrong. It was the situation and timing that caused the misunderstanding. Don't dwell on it now; I've moved on, and you should too. No grudges." He shook hands with her.

Dorothy then asked, "I can't undo the past, but is there anything I can do for you?"

Dr. Hart thought for a moment and said, "There's one thing. Like Inspector Charles did, call the press and tell them I'm innocent—that I did nothing wrong. Say it was all a misunderstanding that led to me being treated like a criminal. If you have to, make up a story to support it. Clearing my name might help me get my medical license back. Do this if you can."

Dorothy agreed enthusiastically. "I'll do it for sure," she said, looking relieved.

"Give me your bank details, and I'll repay the favour."

"There's no need for that." Dorothy answered with a soft expression.

Hearing all this, I couldn't believe what I had just witnessed. Did this mean the *"Innocent"* story wasn't real, but fabricated for a purpose? Why did Inspector Charles lie—was it for money, or was there another hidden reason?

This means that even Doctor Hart, the one person I thought was beyond suspicion, is now back under scrutiny like the others.

Everyone departed, and I made my way to the hospital, but the dilemma remained unchanged: *who's holding the truth, and who's hiding behind deception?*

Stuck in a web of lies, I'm left searching for an exit that doesn't exist.

Merry Christmas

24th December, 1996
10:00 A.M.

The Beardwood Hospital

The clouds loomed overhead, dark and heavy, poised to unleash a torrent of rain. As I entered the dimly lit waiting room, I spotted Leslie, her gaze fixed on the floor, avoiding eye contact. "How's he now?" I asked, in a faint tone.

"I can't say much," Oliver replied, rubbing the sleep from his eyes. "For now, his heart is stable. The doctors did a CT scan—no skull fractures or internal bleeding. There's some swelling, and they may transfer him to Manchester for an MRI if needed."

Leslie's eyes flickered with a mix of hope and exhaustion as she turned to me. "Leslie, he'll be fine. I'll do whatever it takes to make sure of that." I understood the depth of her worry.

"You both should go home. I'll stay here with him,"

I insisted, trying to sound firm.

"I'm not going anywhere. I want to be with him," Leslie replied, her determination unwavering.

Oliver stepped closer, placing a reassuring hand on my shoulder. "I'm here with her, Mr White. You need to go. Ebba needs you."

"Call me if there's an emergency or if you need anything. I'll bring lunch later."

"There's a canteen in the hospital. We'll eat there. You don't have to worry," Oliver replied calmly, though the exhaustion in his voice was undeniable. "And if something urgent comes up, I'll let you know."

I nodded.

As I turned toward Liam's room, my heart pounded. I glanced through the small window. He lay there, motionless, head wrapped in a white surgical bandage, an oxygen mask over his face, the steady beep of the machines the only sign of life.

I closed my eyes, swallowing hard to keep the tears from spilling over. The image of him, so fragile, stayed etched in my mind. Without saying another word, I left. It was difficult to see him in that condition, with the grip of uncertainty settling heavily over me as I stepped out into the darkening day.

11:40 A.M.

The breeze had turned colder, biting through my skin, and a light rain had begun to fall. It was clear that in no time, it would worsen—an ominous sign of the storm that was coming. The sky, dark and brooding, mirrored the terror building inside me.

I stepped into the house, taking in its once—captivating grandeur. Now it felt empty. My obsession with it had dissolved. I no longer wanted to call this place mine.

With heavy shoulders and legs that trembled beneath me, I made my way upstairs, each step echoing in the unnerving silence. I reached Ebba's room, unlocking the door from the outside. As I pushed it open, expecting resistance, the door gave way with ease. My heart skipped a beat. It was already unlocked from the inside.

I stepped into the study. The stress was thick as the storm was brewing outside.

Ebba sat curled in the corner of the room, enveloped in shadows. "Ebba?" I called hesitantly, unsure of what response I would get. She looked up, her eyes wide in the dull light, and after a moment of silence, she asked, "Why did you lock me in?"

Did she not understand the gravity of what had happened?

"I'm hungry, Dad," she said, her voice innocent and sweet.

She seemed unaffected by the chaos that surrounded us, yet I needed to be cautious. "Me too. Come on, let's eat."

With a quiet obedience, she rose and followed me to the dining table.

"Sit. Let me see what we have."

"Where's Mom and Liam?"

Is she testing me, or has she genuinely forgotten the devastation caused by her actions?

"They've gone out. Will be back soon," I replied, keeping my tone even.

"Okay," she said, settling into her chair as I moved to the kitchen.

Knowing her favourites, I prepared black coffee and a cheese omelette, bringing them back to the table. She sat with her head bowed, lost in thought.

"Here you go," I said, placing the food in front of her. She immediately dived in, as if she hadn't eaten in days.

"Delicious! This coffee is better than what Oliver makes, and Mom should learn to cook from you.

Thank you!"

I stood there, watching her eat, her innocence cutting through the turmoil like a knife. In that moment, I realised that the darkness that had overtaken her wasn't truly her—it couldn't be. She would never harm her family.

Once she finished, I took her to her room and helped her settle into bed. She rested her head on my lap as her hair was gently stroked.

"Dad, that book messes with my head. It feels like an addiction—I can't pull myself away from it, no matter how hard I try. Please throw it away, or it'll keep calling me."

Trying to understand what she meant, but within seconds, she was fast asleep. I carefully placed her head on the pillow before leaving quickly for the study room, where the book was thrown in a corner.

The book was picked up and torn to pieces without a second thought, as though all the anger was being taken out on it and blaming it for everything that was happening. It was silly, of course, but in that moment, it felt right.

Returning to Ebba's side, I sat on the bed while leaning against the wall. Heavy eyes refused to close, and sleep wouldn't come. The mind kept racing with endless possibilities.

4:00 P.M.

As I replayed the events in my mind, a knock sounded at the door. I gently moved Ebba to the side of the bed and went to answer it. Oliver stood there, shivering. I stepped aside to let him in. "Why are you here?" I asked, trying to keep my voice steady.

"It's getting cold and also a thunderstorm is on the way. So, I came to get a jacket for ma'am and other essentials," he replied, his teeth chattering.

"You should've called me; I would've come," I said, concerned creeping into my voice.

"I tried, but the weather was messing with the signal."

"It's fine. You go get your jacket, and I'll grab Leslie's."

"Where's Ebba? Is she still...?" Fear flickered in his eyes.

"She's fine for now," I remarked.

"Should I make her a coffee and tea for you?" Oliver suggested.

"No need. You should be with Liam and Leslie. I'll take care of it here."

He nodded slowly; the worry etched on his face.

Gathered what he needed and left, leaving me alone once more with the haunting questions swirling in my mind.

It was Christmas Eve, and I found myself utterly alone. In just one night, everything had spilled out of hand, and I was powerless to stop it. I should've uncovered the dark history of this house long before, yet here I was, piecing it together too late. I should've searched for my father when he vanished instead of losing myself in my own life. Now, I have to act—something, anything—to give meaning to the chaos and to the steps I've taken down this path.

7:00 P.M.

The weather worsens, rain hammering against the windows, punctuated by loud cracks of thunder and gusts of icy wind. I glanced at Ebba, still deep in sleep, her innocent face untouched by the turmoil swirling around us. I sat beside her, lost in thought, reflecting on how different things were last Christmas. All four of us were together, sharing laughter and warmth. Leslie, bustling in the kitchen, crafting puddings and minced pies, while I entertained the kids with tales of Santa and the miracle of Jesus,. with Christmas tunes playing softly in the background. The house felt small, but it was brimmed with joy—something we desperately needed now.

Rising quietly, I slip away to my room, careful not to disturb her slumber. I rummage through my wardrobe, searching for the recorder Liam gifted me.

I need to seize this moment, to embrace the weight of this memory, and remind myself: if I can endure this and stand strong for my family, I can face anything. It's a testament that love outweighs wealth, and when the dust settles, I'll share this recording—with my family.

After a few frustrating minutes, I finally found it, buried under a pile of clothes—a small, unassuming device, yet it holds the power to document my truth. I clutch it tightly and make my way downstairs, the faint sound of rain intensifying outside. I pour myself a drink and can feel the heaviness of the moment resting upon my shoulders. I settle onto the staircase; the wood creaking softly beneath me.

8:30 P.M.

With a shaky breath, I pressed the record button and placed it on my side. The cassette whirs to life, and I began to pour out the raw emotions that have been festering within me, desperate to escape.

'Christmas is just a few hours away, and our family of four is scattered in four different directions. We're not together and it's tearing me apart.

I'm sorry, Leslie, for hiding the truth from you. I was selfish, afraid that sharing the reality would take this place away from us. You don't deserve what you're going through. I can't begin to imagine the pain you're feeling, but I promise, even if you don't want me to, I'll stand by your side and fight to make things right, to bring us back to how we once were. And Leslie, you can hate me, but that won't change the fact that I love you.

My children are also suffering because of me. Every year, they would jump around with excitement, but now, one is unaware of the tragedy that has unfolded, and the other is fighting for his life.'

I wiped my tears, finding it tough to continue.

'Ebba, I know what happened wasn't intentional, and it wasn't your fault. Don't ever feel guilty. We all know how much you love Liam, and your father will always stand by you, no matter what anyone says.
Liam, you're not here with me right now, and I miss you so much. But I know you'll fight through this. You once told me that whenever I feel alone, I should talk to this recorder, as if I am talking to you. I've been trying to follow your advice. I'm trying so hard to be strong, but I keep falling apart. Please, come and hold me. Your daddy needs you.

I love you all, and I hope you can find it in your hearts to forgive me.'

I wanted to say so much more, but I broke down. My hands covered my face as I sobbed, the load of everything finally crashing down. I had been holding it all in for so long, but this time, the dam broke, and the tears came flooding out. The storm outside was nothing compared to the chaos inside me, and I tried to let it all out, wanting to release the pain that had been consuming me.

9:15 P.M.

A knock on the door barely registered in my mind, and I intentionally ignored it, lost in my reflections. Moments later, a thumping sound jolted me from my haze. I wiped my eyes and nose with my sleeve, glancing toward the door as the knock came again—this time, more insistent. I felt a knot tighten in my stomach, expecting Oliver to have forgotten something.

I opened the door, and my breath caught in my throat.

Standing there was a tall, slim man in his fifties, clad entirely in black—from the high-necked, long coat that hung elegantly over his frame to the matching pants and polished shoes. His face was partially obscured by the brim of a hat, casting shadows over his sharp features. He held an umbrella, droplets of rain cascading off it, and wore a pleasant smile that gave me goosebumps.

"Hello, Mr White," he greeted, his grin widening, revealing a glimmer of something unsettling in his eyes.

"Hi, do I know you?" I managed, panic prickling at the back of my mind.
"Yes, you do, and you don't," he replied cryptically,

his words wrapping around my thoughts like tendrils of fog.

'What does that mean?' I wondered.

"Sorry, I didn't get you," I said, trying to mask my growing discomfort.

"Will you not invite me in? It's raining like hell, and I'm all wet." His tone was nonchalant, almost mocking.

I hesitated for a moment, weighing my options, then stepped aside, allowing him to enter. As I closed the door, a loud howl of wind echoed through the house, sending a shiver down my spine—as if the storm were trying to warn me.

"Why is it so dark here? It's Christmas Eve, after all," he remarked, glancing around as he lit the fireplace with calmness that seemed practiced. He shed his coat and hat, placing them aside, and settled comfortably onto the couch.

I took slow, cautious steps toward him, curiosity mingling with dread.

"Is your son dead? No, right? Then why have you made this place a graveyard?" he said, his voice dripping with a strange amusement.

I held up, ice coursing through my veins. How does he know about my son? Who is this man?

"Could you tell me your name, please?" I managed to ask, my voice barely above a whisper.

He met my gaze, calm and unyielding, resting his feet on the table in front of him. The silence stretched, thickening the tension in the room. Finally, he spoke.

"My name is *William Hawkins.*"

As he revealed his identity, thunder rumbled outside, the loudest clap shaking the very foundations of the house, as if the depths of hell were raised in response to his presence.

"What did you just say?" My voice was barely stable, my heart racing as the shock of his words echoed in my mind.

He glanced away, a half-smile playing on his lips. "You heard me, Aston."

It felt impossible. The man who was declared dead twenty years ago was now sitting right in front of me. My mind struggled to catch up, to make sense of the impossible scene unfolding before me.

"If he's alive, then who died that night?" I said to myself, but he caught the question. His reply was swift, brutal.
"Your father."

The words hit me like a punch to the gut. Numb.

As I struggled to process this information, Hawkins scanned the room with a strange fondness in his eyes. "This place... it hasn't changed. You know, Aston, I have so many memories here. Buying this house was my dream, and the day I did, I was the happiest man alive. But then, everything changed... this house robbed me of everything I had."

He rose to his feet and turned to face me, his eyes locked on mine, and began moving closer, each step deliberate, as the space between us shrank, the atmosphere grew heavier, charged with an almost acute distress and instinctively I took a step back. My mind raced, questioning why he was here now, after two decades of silence. His presence, his words, it all felt like a ticking bomb ready to go off. What does he want?

He stopped just inches from me and spoke in an undertone filled with calm. "My story isn't so different from yours, Aston."

Fear tingled at the back of my neck. What had I just walked into?

"You must be wondering why, after all these years, I've stepped out of the shadows," he said, his voice as he circled around me, his presence unnerving with each step.

"Are you a detective, Aston? I was keeping an eye on you through the cracks and I didn't appreciate you digging into a case that was long buried—it pissed me off. And now that I've come to light, there will be repercussions," he murmured. His voice was blunt as he circled closer. "Tonight, you decide—your family or this house. Make no mistake, the choice is yours, but whatever you don't pick... I'll rip it away from you. Choose carefully." His breath brushed against my ear, the threat hanging like a blade over my head.

I twisted my head toward him, meeting his eyes as he smiled and glided across the hall. I stood frozen, unsure of what to say or do, my thoughts scattered. He walked slowly, enjoying the moment.

"Take your time," he said, pausing in the centre of the room. Spreading his arms wide, he closed his eyes as if he was absorbing the essence of the place and reliving his past. "You have two minutes to decide. Until then, let me soak in the atmosphere of my manor," he said, his voice low and alarming, as he remained there with a frightening sense of ownership, as if it were still his.

A deep quietness fell as the seconds ticked by. My mind spun wildly, struggling to keep up with what was happening. It was all too fast, too surreal.

"Time's up, Aston," he said suddenly, still standing in the same pose, eyes closed. "What have you decided?"

I remained quiet, my pulse thundering in my ears.

"Can't hear you," he repeated. "Will it be the house that filled you with an unmatched sense of accomplishment, or will it be Leslie and your children?"

"What if I say both?" I challenged and blurted out, my voice shaky but defiant. Something about his presence, his nerve, filled me with a rebel. I wasn't going to let him dominate me.

His smile faltered. "You know the rules. You can't choose both. Let me remind you, Aston—either this mansion for which you've sacrificed everything, your money, your peace of mind, or the three souls who depend on you. Which is it?"

Ebba is battling her inner turbulence, caught in a storm of emotions; Leslie is dealing with the chaos and somehow holding herself together; my son is facing a life-threatening situation and refusing to surrender; and here I am, allowing this dead man from the past to dictate my thoughts and control me. Not anymore.

"Mr. Hawkins, it's obvious you desire something from me, which is why you're here. So enough with the threats—let's set aside the theatrics and have an actual conversation." I moved ahead, claiming my seat, and he slowly opened his eyes, a smile curling on his lips as he made his way to the couch, settled down across from me.

The rain unleashed its fury; the temperature

dropping sharply, yet I felt no chill. It felt like the upcoming confrontation had lit a fire inside me.

We both studied each other as if any chess game was about to begin, both of us ready to outsmart each other, calculating our moves with deadly precision, each step leading us closer to an inevitable checkmate.

"You went to Grace's house last night, accompanied by Dorothy." he made the opening move

"Oh! So you were the one who followed me."

"There you met Charles and my old friend, Doctor Hart?"

"Friend? Or your killer?" I spat out.

"Yes, both actually. He killed me for twenty years, if not more."

"Why him? He was your friend, and you framed him for your murder."

"I never wanted that for him," he replied, his tone calm, almost amused. "He trapped himself. I did nothing."

"Nothing? You let him take the fall while you watched from the cover of darkness, hidden in plain sight," I countered, anger bubbling beneath the surface.

He bent towards me, his eyes narrowing sharply. "You still don't understand. Sometimes, the greatest betrayals come from those you trust the most."

The storm raged outside; the wind screamed through the night, its fierce wail overwhelming my every sense.

"What are you saying?"

"The biggest mistake George made that night was stepping foot in this house. He made things easier for me—he was never part of the original plan," he said, his tone grave and unflinching.

My eyebrows drew closer. "What was the plan?"

"You have whiskey?" he asked

I nodded, standing without a word. I fetched the bottle and two glasses, poured the amber liquid, then returned to my seat, waiting for the tale, which I was desperate to hear. He raised the glass to his lips, taking a slow sip before slipping into the haze of his memories.

"That night, I sat right where you're sitting now," he began, his voice low but clear. "While drinking, I thought about the perfect way to kill Stella and get away with it."

I felt my pulse quicken; the glass shaking slightly in my hand as I sat fixed. He downed his glass in one gulp, reaching for the bottle to pour himself another, while I remained still, trying to process his cold confession.

"Stella," he continued, eyes distant. "and I got married at a very young age. Out of my love for her, I bought this mansion in her name—a decision I later came to regret.

Everything was perfect at first, except for one thing—we couldn't have a child to complete our family. Years passed, and we tried everything, but nothing worked. Stella grew impatient. The woman who once spent her days in prayer turned her faith to dark rituals. I still remember the day she brought home a book called **The Invitation**. She started performing chanting hexes. I tried to stop her; however, the book was manipulative, pulling her deeper into darkness. She became addicted to it and convinced herself that everything happening was because of it. I knew it was wrong and meaningless, but Stella's desperation to have a child turned into an obsession, and she refused to listen to me.

Not long ago, Bethany and her son, Gerald, moved into the neighbourhood. Stella became friends with her immediately, though I didn't know her true intentions. One day, she said, 'Do you know why we don't have a child?' Before I could answer, she added, 'Because Bethany took him from us. He's trapped with her, and I'm going to bring him back soon.' I found it strange but didn't know what to do.

After that, Gerald, who was introverted and aloof, spent more time in our house than in his own, even with his mother living nearby. Soon, he started calling Stella his mother. Bethany didn't like this and eventually stopped Gerald from seeing Stella completely. That was the turning point.

On the night of December 23rd, 1968, I was away at work when everything went horribly wrong. Stella, overwhelmed by her obsession, lost control. She went to Bethany's house and demanded she give up Gerald. When Bethany refused, Stella stabbed her without a second thought. She died, and Gerald was now Stella's.

When I returned home that night, Carter told me what happened. I was stunned, but knew one thing—I wouldn't let Stella get caught. Darron, who could've been a hurdle, was out of town, which worked in our favour. I went to the crime scene, cleaned up anything that could point back to us, and framed Darron for Bethany's murder. Gerald, quiet and obedient, did exactly what we told him to do. I left him alone in the house with his dead mother to make our story believable. Days later, when Darron returned, I finished the job—he disappeared from everyone's lives forever. We were trying to avoid suspicion, but Stella made it difficult. Every night, she would sneak over to feed Gerald."

"When he said, 'Mother was feeding me,' he meant Stella?" I asked in shock.

Mr. Hawkins nodded and went on. "Afterward, no one came for Gerald—not even his father, Rodrick. But I still wasn't taking chances. I turned Rodrick into another potential suspect because he had a motive. The case was never solved, Darron was gone, and life moved on. Stella's obsession turned me into a murderer, and I hated it. But I can't deny also, it made me feel powerful." He smiled, took a sip of whiskey. "Over time, Stella grew even more attached to Gerald, drifting further away from me. They became nothing more than a burden. Then, in 1973, we got lucky. Arthur was born. I thought having a child would fix everything, bring Stella back to me, but it didn't. The fights only got worse. We were two strangers sharing the same roof. I wanted to put a stop to this—I needed to get rid of Gerald, the outsider in my family but Stella made it clear—she would divorce me, take the house, tear Arthur away from me, and bleed me dry with alimony, leaving me penniless. I'd have nothing left. If I ever dare to come between her and Gerald, I knew she will destroy me without delay. After that threat, all the love I had for her vanished, and I found my next victim."

His words felt like a blade slicing through the air, sharp and deliberate.

"She owned everything—the house, the assets. The only way I could keep it all was to remove her. But I couldn't just assassinate her. People would think I was guilty. I had to take her down in a way that no one would suspect, not even Stella. I needed to make it appear as though she was losing her sanity."

The room felt smaller, darker. I watched him refill his glass, his hand steady, as if he wasn't unravelling a nightmare. He took a longer sip this time, continuing with the same mysterious calm.

"I began giving her Scopolamine, also known as *Devil's Breath*. At first, just a small amount—something subtle. But over time, I increased the doses. The brilliance of that drug is its ability to leave no trace. It affects the mind, not the body. No one could see what I was doing." He gave a bitter smile. "And as her condition worsened, I kept her away from hospitals, only allowing doctors I trusted—my friends—into the picture. That way, I could easily manipulate them. They never doubted a thing. As she spiralled deeper, they stayed blind to it all. No one questioned what was happening to her."

I downed my whiskey in one quick swallow, my throat tightening—not from thirst, but through the impact of his every word. Each sentence seemed to suck the air out from the room, leaving me with a dry mouth and a mind reeling in disbelief. The walls seemed to close in, and I couldn't tell what disturbed me more: the cold precision of his confession or the fact that I was still sitting there, listening, instead of alerting others and exposing him.

"Okay, you wanted to kill her because you knew she would have to go to the hospital after Christmas, and then you'd be exposed." I asked in a dull tone.

"Right, but there's more to it."

"And what's that?"

He leaned back, a grin flickering across his face. "Stella shifted her focus and priority, and so did I. She pushed me away, and in time, I found someone else. I fell in love. To be with her, I had to kill Stella."

"What?" I asked in a startled voice.

A knock echoed through the room, loud and relentless. I paid no attention, my gaze locked on him. I asked, "With whom?"

He didn't answer, savouring his drink like he had all the time in the world. The knock came again, louder this time. My heart raced as I hurried to the door. Hawkins remained seated, completely unfazed, almost as if he already knew exactly who was on the other side.

As I opened it, another surprise awaited me.

"Dorothy?" I barely recognised her, standing on the doorstep transformed. She wore a sleek royal blue puffer jacket zipped tight, black jeans that clung to her legs, and knee-high boots that exuded confidence. The fragile figure I once knew was no longer in sight. The torn clothes and weary lines etched on her face had been replaced by an aura of elegance and vitality.

"Mr. White," she acknowledged with a nod as she stepped inside, leaving me momentarily confused. She closed her umbrella with a speedy motion and shut the door behind her.

Then she walked over to Mr Hawkins, perching herself on the armrest of his couch. They shared a kiss, and it took me a few seconds to grasp the shocking reality: she was the woman he had fallen in love with.

Somehow, I slumped back into my seat, feeling their predatory eyes fixate on me. Mr. Hawkins picked up right where he had left off.

"She used to come over to babysit, and during that time, we became deeply attached—partners in crime. She was the one who gave the first dose of Devil's Breath, and that's where it all began. As time went by, me and Dorothy grew closer. When she became pregnant, she had no choice but to leave town, seeking refuge elsewhere until the baby arrived. I was eager to proclaim to the world that I had become a father, the joy swelling within me, but Stella was the only obstacle preventing me from revealing anything.
So, I had two reasons to finish her off."

I paused for a moment, tried to make sense of everything, then asked, "Why did you kill my father? What did he do?"

"Carter was always by Stella's side, his loyalty to her surpassing mine," he replied, his tone chilling. "He was becoming suspicious. Somehow, he figured out I was behind Stella's deteriorating mental state. I had entrusted him with giving her the medication, which was actually that drug. He acted on my instructions for a while, but then started looking for excuses to stop. That fool was overstepping by refusing to follow my orders. That indicated he had too much knowledge and could become a liability."

Each of his words felt like shards of glass piercing my heart, igniting a fierce anger deep within me. Justice will be served, Mr Hawkins, the murderer of my father, but I knew that now was not the time. I had to maintain my composure, to play the role of the helpless hostage while he rejoiced in his perceived power. By giving him the illusion that he was in control, I aimed to uncover the truth hidden beneath his tangled lies.

"I've heard everyone else's version—now, I want yours." I pushed him, hoping he'd reveal more. "How did you pull it off so smoothly, killing two innocent people and getting away with it?"

He exchanged a quick glance with Dorothy, and they both laughed, as if I'd just paid him a compliment. Then he spoke, "It all got possible because of the senseless morons and the twist of fate; without them, it would've been much harder."

"What do you mean by that?" I queried.

"The night of 23rd December 1976, I set out to get the drugs, but halfway there, I changed my mind. Realised that before the night ended, I'd get rid of Stella, cancelling the need for the drugs entirely. My second target was Carter. The plan was simple and unchanged: just as Bethany was killed and Darron, the main suspect, was never seen again, this time Stella would step into Bethany's role, and Carter would take on the part of Darron.

My first course of action was I would go to George, making sure he would vouch for me later, proving I was with him when everything went down. Everyone would believe I was just a loving husband, out getting medicine for his mentally unstable wife, who tragically ended up dead—slayed by a servant. A servant who, conveniently, disappeared with all the money."

"But in reality, he will be 4 feet under the ground, hidden in the woods," Dorothy added with a giggle.

"But then, three new problems stared me down. First, what to do with Grace? She wasn't part of the original plan, and now I had to decide fast. While I was still figuring that out, I invited that fool George over for a drink, just like old times. I couldn't have made a worse choice. It left me with even less time to pull everything off. And then there was my final headache: how to wipe out Carter and lay his body to rest in the forest without anyone speculating a thing.

But as fate would have it, on my way back, I saw Grace running in panic, heading in the opposite direction. It was as if the universe was handing me the perfect solution.

At 12:15 A.M., I parked my car outside and went straight to her," he said, glancing at Dorothy as his hand rested on her thigh. "I needed her help to finish the job. We went inside and found Carter pounding on the door. I asked her to stay in the hall to guard the door. I rushed upstairs, seeing the dismay etched on Carter's face. Blood streaked the doorframe as he stammered that Stella had locked herself in the children's room—with a knife. Everything was falling apart, spiralling out of control in a way I hadn't anticipated. Carter and I slammed ourselves against the door, and after a few frantic hits, it finally gave way.

The room was shrouded in darkness. Stella stood by the crib, her white nightgown drenched in red, a knife clutched in her hand, a demonic look on her face as she growled in aggression. Gerald was lying motionless in the corner, eyes tightly closed, petrified with fear. I stepped inside and saw Arthur—his tiny body drained of blood. My little boy was dead. And on Stella's face, there wasn't a hint of regret. She has never been particularly close to Arthur. She spoke with a composed, detached tone, uttering the words that made me snap: 'He was responsible for my suffering. He was evil and had to die. I should've killed him the day he was born.'

I stretched out my arms, gripping her neck, and slammed her against the wall. My rage swelled with every second, tightening my hold. Carter shouted for me to stop, but he didn't dare to get close. As I choked the life out of her, she lashed out in desperation, stabbing me twice—but I felt nothing. I didn't loosen my grip, not for a second, and I watched as the light faded from her eyes. Aston, I can't begin to describe how satisfying it was."

It was painfully clear that he felt no guilt, cherishing every moment as he recounted his sins with a twisted sense of pleasure.

"She crumpled to the floor as I released her neck, turning back to Arthur. I kissed his cold forehead, taking a deep breath to embrace the finality, and then checked on Gerald, who was still alive. I was ready to end him right then, but he wasn't on my list of targets. So, I decided to take a risk and not harm him, given his history of staying mute, anyway. On top of that, he was enduring acute stress disorder, which neutralised any danger he might pose.

I locked away my emotions, wrapping them in a calm mask, and ordered Carter to drag Stella out and stash it in the study room. He hesitated for a moment, but then complied. It wasn't just time slipping away; I was losing blood fast, and I needed to shift my strategy before it was too late. I had intended to burn the body, but there wasn't enough time, so I had to delay it.

After that, we both descended the stairs. Dorothy came to me, gently taking my hand and guiding me to the couch as blood seeped from my wounds. She rushed upstairs for the first aid kit, but my vision blurred, and staying conscious was a battle. The ever-present fear of George and the police showing up at any time consumed me, suffocating every thought. The stress mounted, overwhelming my senses. As darkness closed in around me, I lost control and collapsed on the floor, unconsciously." Mr Hawkins stopped, reached into his pants pocket, and retrieved a pack of cigarettes.

Dorothy continued, picking up where he had left. "In the next few minutes George was here and found him sprawled on the floor. I hid, biding my time, waiting for the perfect moment to strike."

"I thought he would jeopardise the entire plan. Instead, he gave us an escape route—leaving behind proof of his presence."

"So, you were the one who—" Before I could finish my question, she cut me off.

"Yes, I was the one who attacked Dr Hart. After he was down, it all became easier. Carter and I went directly to the study to wrap up the unfinished business."

Placing his glass down, Mr. Hawkins grabbed two cigarettes from the pack and offered one to Dorothy. She asked, "Got a lighter?"

"Yes," I said, handing it to her.

They both placed the cigarette between their lips, and she flicked the lighter, igniting the tips. She inhaled deeply, briefly closing her eyes as exhaled a thin stream of smoke.

"Your father gave me the matchbox that night," she continued, the cigarette bobbing between her fingers. "I had to make sure her life was over. So, I lit my cigarette, taking my time, and poured the alcohol over Stella's body. I stood there, took a slow drag, staring at her one last time. Then, took a second drag—and it was time to end it. I flipped the cigarette, watched it arc through the air, and the moment it touched her, she went up in flames. The fire caught fast, consuming her in seconds. It was strangely beautiful, watching her burn. Immediately after, we hurried to check on him." She extended her hand in a motion toward Mr Hawkins.

He tossed the cigarette filter to the ground and crushed it under his foot. Relaxed in one spot, enjoying every nuance of the tale. An unnatural quiet overtook the room, broken only by the steady drumming of rain against the windows.

"Carter rushed to his room and emerged moments later. 'I have to leave; Grace will show up with the police any minute.' Carter said in a subdued voice while standing there, with bags gripped tightly in his hands. Every shiver of his body showed how scared he was." She pointed toward Oliver's room, the same one that had belonged to my father twenty years ago.

"I could feel the urgency in his words, but deep down, I knew I couldn't let him leave. He had to die—there was no other choice. If he got away, he would be the reason for our downfall.

Meanwhile, I looked him over from head to toe, and something struck me—his build. It was almost similar to Mr Hawkins. Same height, body type and skin tone. At that moment, I knew exactly what I needed to do. But Carter was already heading toward the front door, and I had to stop him.

'You can't just leave like this!' I shouted.

He paused, turning back to me. 'By now, the flames must be visible for miles. I can't afford to get caught. My family's waiting—I have to disappear before it's too late.'

'No one's getting caught, Carter. Fine, if you want to leave, go ahead. But at least help me with Mr Hawkins, or he's going to die here tonight, too.'

The hesitation flickered in his eyes. My words worked. Slowly, he dropped his bags and hung his head, then set them aside.

'We don't have time,' he muttered. 'I will stop the bleeding. You go get some water.'

I didn't wait. I bolted to the kitchen and rushed back. Sprinkled it on Hawkins' face, I watched as his eyelids fluttered open. In no time, he was back to his senses, but still in severe pain.

Carter bandaged Mr. Hawkins' wounds, helping him sit up as he offered him water. I seized the moment to dash upstairs, returning before anyone noticed my absence.

I stood behind him, hands clasped tightly behind my back. "Now, I think you should go, Carter."

He turned to me, resting Mr. Hawkins' head against the wall before standing. 'He's safe for now. You both should leave, too. I'm going to my family and I'll never come back. Don't worry, I won't say a word about this.'

'I will make sure of that," I replied. With calculated precision, I plunged the knife into his stomach, right where Mr Hawkins had been stabbed. I pulled it out and plunged it in again. That bitch stabbed my love twice, so I had to do the same. Dr Hart found two wounds on Mr Hawkins, and if there was only one on this body, it could come back to haunt us."

A sinister chuckle escaped from Dorothy, resonating through the hall, soon joined by Mr Hawkins. Their laughter echoed around us, a haunting symphony of madness.

I wiped the tears from the corners of my eyes;

hearing all this about my father was excruciating. Even if he weren't my father, the brutality of it all was still unimaginable. Yet here were these two psychopaths in front of me, devoid of any grief or regret.

"There's more to it—listen," Mr. Hawkins began, suppressing a laugh. "At first, I had no idea why she did what she did. But when she told me to switch clothes with him, it all became clear—I wasn't just giving him my clothes, I was giving him my identity too. I paid careful attention to every small detail, making sure not a single thing slipped past me. At that moment, Dorothy calmly wiped her fingerprints from the knife, then pressed Carter's hand against the handle, leaving his prints behind. She tucked the knife into the corner, disguising it skilfully. Then I doused Carter in alcohol, struck a match from his own box, and set him ablaze. Before we left the house to start our new life, I ensured the body was burned beyond 80% to make it unrecognisable and eliminate any trace of fingerprints. To top it off, neither of us had dental records, making the plan foolproof."

"It's a good thing that DNA analysis didn't exist back then," Dorothy remarked, struggling to suppress a grin.

"Even if it had, it wouldn't have mattered," Mr Hawkins replied. "George unknowingly helped us. He was caught just hours after the killings, which was an unexpected twist in our favour."

He downed his sixth glass, while my second still sat untouched. He set the empty glass on the table with a deliberate clink.

"That's how everything came together, letting me walk free and I kept myself hidden until this day," he said. "That night, luck was on my side. Grace took the long route to the police, George—he shouldered the blame, walking straight into a trap that wasn't meant for him. Carter was there to take my place."

I stared at him, barely able to contain my rage. Dorothy rose from her seat, walking to the window. Without turning around, she spoke, her voice detached. "The rain's slowing. We should leave soon. Wrap this up quickly."

Hawkins smirked, his eyes locking onto mine. "The disappointment in your eyes is clear, Aston. I could say sorry for your loss, but I won't. This isn't about apologies, it's about taking more. So, tell me—this house, or your family?"

I couldn't let him win again. He couldn't be that lucky.

"Family," I answered, my voice strong and confident.

"Oh, great!" he said, springing to his feet with excitement. "You're on a two-month deadline to transfer the house to Dorothy and leave."

"Not going anywhere from here." I started, leaning

back in my chair, calmly settling over me. "I will always prioritise my family above everything else, but you can try taking this house from me if you dare."

He paused, standing still for a moment, before sitting back down, his expression shifting.

"You know you can't—" he began, but I cut him off.

"I can see the frustration, Mr. Hawkins. But I'm curious now, what can you do? I'll take both—the house and my family. So, what's your next move? Kill me too? And who will you swap my identity with this time?"

Dorothy turned and came back. She hadn't expected me to challenge them. Mr. Hawkins remained silent for a moment before rising to his feet.

I asked in an aggressive tone. "Tell me one thing. What if I kill you right now? Killing a dead man isn't a crime, is it?"

Mr. Hawkins chuckled darkly, unfazed. "Ahh, Aston, I expected better from you. Your battle isn't with me," he said, his voice low and deliberate. "The real danger comes from within your own circle."

Before I could grasp his meaning, he continued, his tone cold and measured. "It's good to see you're willing to fight back, and I don't fault you for it. But now that you know my secrets, understand that

I also know far more about you and your family than anyone else ever could. This isn't personal, Aston. But this house—*my* house—was never yours. It belongs to Dorothy and my son."

"Which son, Mr. Hawkins?" I shot back, my voice edged. "Arthur, who's dead, or Gerald, locked away in an asylum for the past two decades?"

A slow, creepy smile crept across his face. "My third son, Oliver."

"Oliver?" I repeated, my heart sinking.

"Yes, he's the Trojan horse," Hawkins said, his voice dripping with satisfaction.

Their laughter began to bubble up, dark and twisted, as I sank deeper into my seat. "But I must apologise on his behalf. What happened with Liam and Ebba could have been avoided." He stepped closer, placing a hand on my shoulder, catching my eye.

"Oliver was so captivated by my stories that he himself wanted to see the effects of drugs. So, he started slipping them into your daughter's morning coffee. Slowly, the signs began to show—and soon enough, it became life-threatening for Liam."

Before I could digest the betrayal, I realised, "He's with Leslie and Liam," I stammered, fear gripping me as I got to my feet..

"Relax, Aston," Hawkins murmured, his voice a serpent's whisper. "They're safe... *for now*. Oliver won't act without my command."

He slipped on his coat, adjusted his hat with exactness, and grabbed the umbrella with a final, purposeful motion. "It's time for us to leave. You've got a couple of months to do what needs to be done. If not, I'll personally dig three graves—for your entire family.
They will rest in peace, but you will not."

He cast a quick glance at Dorothy over his shoulder, and she nodded slightly. The task was given.

Dorothy meticulously wiped away the fingerprints from the bottle and glass. Then she bent down, snatching the cigarette filter from the floor and slipping it into her pocket, her movements swift and practiced. With every action, she ensured that not a trace of evidence remained, the thrill of the game fuelling her determination.

"I expect some maturity from you, Aston," Mr. Hawkins said, his voice eerily composed. "Don't go out there and make a fool of yourself by telling people about me. I'll vanish into thin air again, and without proof, your claims are worthless. You understand what you need to do now. It's over for you. Goodbye, and hope we never cross paths again."

The clock struck midnight, its chime echoing through the hall. The sharp crackle of firecrackers pierced the night, each burst cutting through the silence.

"Merry Christmas, Aston. I hope next year you celebrate this with your family," he added with a demonic grin before turning and walking out the door with Dorothy.

I rushed to close the door behind them, slamming it shut and stood there, staring at the locked door, trying to absorb the moment.

I slowly made my way back to the staircase and sank down onto the steps. I picked up the recorder and pressed the *STOP* button, a small smile creeping onto my face.

"Merry Christmas, Mr. Hawkins," I whispered, my voice laced with quiet vengeance and satisfaction. "I will pray to god that you get what you deserve and it's far from over. See you soon." I spoke softly into the still air, the words laced with dark satisfaction.

25th February, 1997
10:00 P.M.

"When's Oliver coming back? It's hard to keep things under control without him," Leslie said, stepping out of the kitchen.

I avoided her question and her stare, picking up the newspaper from the table, the soft hum of the radio filling the hall.

"How many times are you going to read that paper today?"

"One last time. Are the kids asleep?" I asked, settling onto the couch.

"Yes, they are. Come to bed, it's late."

"I'll be up in a bit. You go ahead," I replied, wanting to read the article one more time."

Alright, but switch off the radio. Liam might wake up." She said and headed upstairs to the bedroom.

I leaned forward and switched off the radio, plunging the house into suffocating silence. Unfolding the newspaper, I scanned the headline again, feeling the happiness settling in.

The Hawkins' Manor

The town's grandest mansion is once again in the spotlight. After twenty years, the long-forgotten murder case is being reopened.According to Inspector Charles Ashford, Dr. George Hart may not be the true culprit. Fresh evidence has emerged. An audio recording has been presented in court, leading the judges to order a full reinvestigation. The real killer is now the target.

There are several speculations:

First, that this could be connected to Bethany's murder case.

Second, that Carter and Darron aren't missing, but are actually dead.

And lastly, a drug known as Devil's Breath was used, a substance capable of destroying one's psyche, pushing them to the brink of insanity, with lifelong repercussions.

By: Aston White, Journalist

—

I tucked the paper slowly, set it aside, and leaned back. Closing my eyes, I let a faint smile creep across my face as the taste of victory washed over me. I was lost in my own world when I heard it again—a low, a disturbing murmur that sent shivers coursing through my body.

"The days are drowned beneath the murky sky,
And nights are choked with fear.

This place is nothing but a pit of dark,
A lair where none should dare.

If you've come, you've sealed your fate,
Your death is lurking near.

They'll crouch on your grave and laugh aloud,
Your soul is bound to them, forever here."

Panic surged through me as I leapt to my feet, rushing to check the radio; it was off. But as I turned, I froze. There stood Ebba on the staircase, her dead eyes fixed on me. The chant came in a voice that echoed with a terrifying, distant resonance.

"Is this the end?" I asked myself.

"No, it's just the beginning of something far worse." Came the response from within.